broken water

a novel-in-stories

paula martin morell

Temenos Publishing * Little Rock, AR

Cover art by Mitchell Crisp Patterson.

ISBN 0-9785648-2-0

$\mathcal{T}$emenos Publishing * Little Rock, AR
www.temenospublishing.com

for jas

Acknowledgements

Thank you: to all of you I've had the privilege of working with in my workshops and classes; to Allison and Paula, for your incredible insight and lifetimes of friendship; to Karen and Al, for being my sister and brother and for showing me what true courage is; to Mom for your kindness and love; to Dad and Mary Jane for your loving support; to Annaliese and Sophia, for picking me to be your mother; and to Jas, for being You.

Namaste,

Paula M. Morell, July 2004

"Overlapping" was originally published in *Short Story Journal*, "Bait" was originally published in *The Little Rock Free Press*, and "Going Deaf," "Riches to Keep," "The Channel" and "Pieces of Me" were originally published in *New Works Review*.

6

ellie

bait

My brother Toby thinks he's been abducted by aliens. Twice. It's embarrassing, really, the way he's been carrying on for the past couple of years, joining Abductees Anonymous, his pilgrimages to Roswell, taping the "X Files" every Sunday and watching it again and again all week long. Of course, I'm the only one he talks this nonsense to besides other abductees. Lucky me. I've tried calmly to tell him there is no such thing as an alien life-force, tried to explain to him that Roswell is not a government cover-up, tried to convince him that all the TV shows about extraterrestrials are just greedy people feeding off the fears of the masses about the end of the millennium. But he doesn't listen to reason. He just brushes me off and tells me that when the aliens finally do make their presence known to the world, and bring peace and goodwill to mankind, I'll be left behind when they take the believers to a better place. Call me crazy, but I would rather sit right here on good old Earth than be carried off to some strange world against my will.

The vent over my head blows thin, cool air through the room as I wait for Toby in the art deco lobby of WebGraphics. Toby's office is on the fifteenth floor of the tallest building in downtown Little Rock. Someone once told me that casinos pump oxygen through the air vents to keep the gamblers awake and alert. I don't know about that, but I wouldn't doubt that Mr. Hanson, the owner of WebGraphics, does the same thing, keeping his twentysomething web page designers full of oxygen to make him more money.

I shift on the lime green chair, the skin on the back of my thighs sticking to the vinyl. It's a warm day for December, so warm that I'm wearing my faded cut-offs and black Converse. There's something about wearing summer clothes in the dead of winter, as if you're defying nature, somehow. I'm sure this warm weather won't stay for long. Hell, it'll probably be freezing by tomorrow. But for right now I want to enjoy the warm sunshine while it lasts.

Beatrice, Toby's secretary, peers over her spectacles at me, then looks back down at her *Good Housekeeping*. Beatrice must be pushing seventy. I know she doesn't like me. Ever since Toby started working here I've made surprise visits like this to take him out in the sunshine. He spends entirely too much time chained to his computer, and sometimes weeks go by when the only daylight he sees is through his office window. I don't have a problem with Toby being a hard worker. Hell, I bartend five nights a week at the White Water Tavern. Everybody has to make a buck. What I have a problem with is his being twenty-five and working sixty or seventy hours a week. He's my little brother, and he needs to have fun sometimes.

Behind Beatrice's desk, the door to Toby's office slowly opens. He sticks his head out just far enough for the light to catch his gleaming scalp. Toby shaves his head every morning and then rubs baby oil over the smooth skin. Says hair just gets in the way of thinking, cuts off oxygen to the brain. I have no idea what he is talking about, as I have shoulder-length hair and think just fine. But, then again, Toby seems to be getting plenty of oxygen here at the office. Maybe if he got out of here long enough he would see that hair would help protect him from the oxygen, keep him from going crazy with thinking. Too much thinking can't be good for anyone.

Toby's deep brown eyes land on mine, and he brings his finger up to touch his lips. Beatrice is still staring at her magazine, so Toby inches the door open, stoops down, and then places something on the faux tile floor. At first I can't see what it is, but then I hear a faint clicking noise and a small wind-up alien wearing red tennis shoes comes walking across the floor. It has deep black sockets for eyes, long, thin arms with bulbous hands at the ends, and a protruding belly button. I try not to laugh out loud as the alien marches up to Beatrice, its smooth, white head bouncing up and down, up and down. Toby stands back up as Beatrice looks sideways at the alien, pushes her spectacles up her nose, and then goes back to her magazine. As the alien runs head-on into Beatrice's desk leg, Toby steps out of the door and his whole face breaks into a smile. There's nothing quite like Toby's smile.

"Hey, Ellie, what's up? You've come to rescue me from this hellhole, save me from the evil Beatrice?"

Toby is wearing his favorite Darth Vader T-shirt, black jeans, and combat boots. His shirt reminds me of the days we would ride our bikes to Breckenridge Theater and crouch down in the overstuffed seats so that we could watch *Star Wars* over and over again. Toby was always fascinated with Darth, the epitome of the dark side, and when it was revealed that Darth was Luke Skywalker's father in *The Empire Strikes Back*, Toby cried for two days. I don't know why he was so surprised. I saw it coming all along. I guess Toby just wanted to believe that Darth was totally evil, and there was no way a Jedi could turn out so bad.

I stand up from the vinyl chair. "You got it, brother. I'm here to take you away. The sun is shining, it's above seventy degrees, and Murray Park awaits us. Get your Frisbee and let's get out of here."

Toby reaches inside his office door and pulls out his black Frisbee. As he walks past Beatrice and stoops down to pick up the alien, he says, "If Mr. Hanson asks, I'll be back late this afternoon. You have yourself a nice afternoon, Beatrice. I'll see you around four." Beatrice never even looks up.

I turn to head out of the lobby, suddenly irritated with Toby because he thinks he has to come back at all. I know Toby, and I know that he can afford to take an afternoon off. Hell, last year he made forty-thousand dollars. That's more than I make in two years. But I know it's not the money that Toby cares about. He lives in a small apartment, drives a beat-up '72 Landcruiser, and still wears his favorite T-shirts from high school. I even suspect he gives a lot of his money away to research on extraterrestrial life. No, it's some strange drive that keeps Toby working so hard all the time, as if he has to prove to everyone that he really is worth something.

God, I've got to get out of here. This oxygen is getting to me. As I reach for the door, I hear the faint clicking noise behind me. I turn around just in time to see Toby running up behind me as the alien marches its way across Beatrice's desk.

Murray Park is a chunk of land that sits on the edge of the Arkansas River, just downstream from Murray Lock and Dam. For some reason, the city planners decided to put in a huge parking lot and pavilions and call this place a park. I have to admit, with all the open space it's a great place to throw a Frisbee, but the river is so murky you can't even see your hand under the surface, and the current is so bad that two people died last summer when they fell in. On a sunny Saturday in the summer there may be a hundred or so people here, barbecuing, playing hacky sac, or just lying around on blankets. But today there is only a tattooed couple in an El Camino and an old man picking up cans. Toby and I sit beside each other on a cement picnic table a couple of yards from the swirling river.

Toby is tying a red bandanna on his head to keep his scalp from getting sunburned. It's strange to see Toby from this angle, with his hands behind his neck, his eyes closed. For some reason he looks like Dad right now, wrinkles around his eyes from squeezing them closed with concentration, his lips thin and flat in a straight line. I've never seen him like this. He's always looked young to me, the ten-year-old who would tag along with me and my friends to the strip-mall arcade on Saturday morning. I look away from Toby and to the river as he finishes tying the knot.

"Hey Ellie," he says, "know what I heard?"

I turn back to him, relieved that he is back to looking like the Toby I know. "I have no idea. What can possibly top the 'fact' that Linda Tripp is a man?"

Toby smiles, his eyes lighting up around the edges. "Okay, okay, that one was a little questionable. Not that it's not true. Just that the validity of the charge is a little shaky. I did get that from www.IhateTripp.com, so there may be some bias going on. But what I heard about the catfish in the river is true, because I heard it from a guy who has seen it first-hand."

I look down to the table and pick up the Frisbee. Suddenly I don't want to hear any more of this story. Toby is so naive and gullible sometimes. He thinks just because someone tells you something that it has to be true. It's usually fun to listen to Toby's stories. But today I don't want to hear how he believes someone's tall tale.

"Why don't we throw the Frisbee?" I ask as I stand up from the table. If I can stop this conversation now, then maybe there won't be any more stories for the rest of the afternoon. But Toby isn't giving up that easily.

"There are catfish in this river as big as a Volkswagen Bug. Bigger than 250 pounds. So big that this guy John who was a diver on the construction crew for the I-430 bridge said that when they dove down to lay the concrete, they thought they ran into some kind of underwater monster. He said they couldn't even keep a crew, those damn fish were so big. Could swallow a man in one bite. Like that guy Jonah and the whale."

I take the Frisbee and throw it as far as I can to my right, the black disc floating through the air and landing on the lifeless grass. "That story about Jonah is just that: a story," I say as I turn back to him. "You're not supposed to believe it happened."

Toby stares at the river like I'm not even here. "I just I wish I could see one of those catfish myself. I would jump down his throat and tickle his tonsils until he spit me right back here on the shore."

I step in front of him, but he won't look at me. Then I grab his elbow. His eyes meet mine.

"There's no obese man-eating catfish dwelling in this river or any river," I say, my voice thick like mud. "It's all a joke. A joke on you. You're just crazy enough to believe it."

Toby looks away from me and to the river. I can see anger spreading upward from his neck to his ears like thin, red paint. I haven't seen him like this since Dad told us he was leaving Mom the day Toby graduated from high school.

Suddenly my hand drops from his elbow. I am such an idiot. I wish I hadn't unloaded on him. I am practically the only friend he has. He hasn't talked to Dad since last Christmas, and he avoids Mom like the plague. The only people he communicates with on a regular basis are fellow abductees in chat rooms. The other guys at the office never invite him to lunch, and Beatrice acts like he doesn't exist.

Toby takes two steps toward the river and then whirls back around to me. The way his eyes are glaring at me he could have just as well slapped me in the face. I feel the sting in both my cheeks as I try to stay calm, try not to hurt Toby's feelings any more than I already have. My mind races, trying to find the words that will make this all seem better.

Toby's mouth opens once and then closes back into a thin line. The anger has now consumed his face and is bleeding into his red bandanna. I swear I can see his heart pounding under Darth's helmet.

He reaches up, pulls off the bandanna, and runs it across his forehead. Then the strangest thing happens. The color in Toby's face just drains away, as if someone pulled the plug. His eyes never leave mine. He puts the bandanna into his jeans pocket and shrugs. "Maybe I am crazy. Or maybe I just want to believe. At least I believe in something. You don't believe in anything, Ellie. Not even yourself."

Toby turns and walks to the river. I have no idea what to say. Okay, it's true that I don't believe in most things. As a matter of fact, I can't think of one thing right now that I do believe in that I can't prove to be true. But that's normal, isn't it? Don't most people have to have proof of things before they spend their time and energy on them?

I watch as Toby sits down on the riverbank, pulls off his boots and socks, and submerges his feet in the ice-cold water. As I walk over to pick up the Frisbee, I'm struck with how strange it is that Toby and I have turned out so different. We played with the same toys, ate the same food, and learned the same lessons, yet we try to live in the world in different ways. Toby is right-- he believes in everything; I believe in nothing. I don't know who's worse off.

The Frisbee is smooth in my hands as I pick it up, the black plastic warm from the afternoon sun. As I walk toward Toby, I see a stick poking out of the ground. It comes easily out of the dirt as I pull it up. Right before I get to Toby, I stop, bend down, and pull the laces out of one of my tennis shoes. Then I tie one end of my shoelace onto the end of the stick.

I sit down on the riverbank, my shoulder grazing Toby's. He turns to look at me. I can see his smile out of the corner of my eye as I hold the stick out over the river, but I don't turn to him. I keep my eyes on the water.

After a moment Toby turns back to the water, but I know that that smile is still there. I can feel it mingling with mine in the reflection. There is silence between us as I lower the stick toward the water. The shoelace skims the surface, the murky brown water rippling in circles spreading outward.

going deaf

Tom stands erect in front of his symphony orchestra, his ebony tails fluttering behind him as his body trembles with anticipation. His eyes are closed as they always are, his black hair glistening in the bright lights, a thin line of sweat beading above his upper lip. For a moment there is a hush of silence that falls like a velvet curtain, and then Tom's hands rise, pause, and jerk four times with splayed fingers. The orchestra bursts out four ominous notes in C Minor-- and stops with the punctuation of Tom's closing fingers. Again, silence, and then again Tom's hands wrench from the orchestra the four haunting notes as if Fate is knocking at the door. Silence, with the punctuation of his fingers. With the nod of his head the violins begin their lonely cry as the cornets, piccolo, flutes and oboes pick up the haunting movement. Tom creates the music as the harmonies and melodies blend together and course through his body as if they are his breath, his life. The music swells and falls, lives and breathes, whispers a story of tragedy that transforms into triumph in the C Major fanfare of the finale. Every cell in Tom's body pulsates, harmonizes, with the music. He pulls the notes out of the air with his hands and then puts them back with his breath. He forgets where he is as the orchestra performs and tears run down his cheeks. The symphony is him, and he is the symphony.

I don't know why Dad insists on inviting me over every year for Christmas Eve dinner. He's been doing this ever since he and Mom got divorced eight years ago. He's on wife number four, Candace, who's about my age, twenty-eight. Every year I drive across Little Rock to the house I grew up in for our one visit of the year, and every year Dad ends up barely saying a word to me and then leaving me alone with the wife du jour. Right after dinner Dad will mumble something about making a phone call and then stand up from the table and walk down the hallway to his den. The only thing I hear from behind the closed door is the crackling of the fire in the stone fireplace. And I'm stuck cleaning the kitchen with a stranger. I don't know why Dad disappears sometimes for over an hour. I can only guess he wants me to become buddies with the current woman in his life. My brother Toby gave up trying last year. Says Dad just invites us to make himself feel better. I guess I'm sitting here in Dad's house again this year because I haven't learned my lesson yet.

We're sitting at Dad's antique cherry wood dining table, the same table at which we would eat Sunday dinner when I was growing up. Candace's eyes stare at me from over the top of her gold-rimmed wine glass as she sips her white Zinfandel, her eyelashes thick and black like spiders, the tiny Christmas trees painted on the tips of her scarlet fingernails curling around the glass. Her rhinestone Rudolf sweatshirt shoots rainbows through the room with every breath she takes.

Dad is sitting at the head of the table now, wearing his usual khaki pants and powder blue button-down that looks like it's so stiff it could stand up on its own. He's a tall man, about 6'4", and skinny as a beanpole. People tell me I look just like Mom when she was my age, thick auburn hair and dark brown eyes. But I'm tall and thin like Dad. We even have the same ears. Of course, his have tufts of gray hair, so I wouldn't say we have the exact same ears. But they have the same long lobes and pointed tops. We even have the same freckle on the bottom of the left lobe.

For some reason Dad thinks he can comb three strands of hair across the top of his head and everyone will think he still has his hair. I don't know who he's trying to convince more, himself or everyone else. I would think that by the time you're fifty you would just give up trying to hold onto your youth, give into the fact that you'll never be twenty years old again. But not my dad. I think he's convinced that he's getting younger every year. He even has the red Corvette to prove it.

I know Candace is staring at me, but I don't feel like making small talk. It's strange to sit at this table and eat off someone else's china and try to choke down something I'm supposed to call "mom's" butterbeans. For twelve years Toby and I sat at this table alone for dinner--without Dad because he was at the office, without Mom because she was in the kitchen. Dad didn't come home until after ten-thirty or so, when we were already into "The Tonight Show." Mom waited until we were finished eating and then cleared the table and ate by herself at the breakfast table in the kitchen. When Dad came home he would pick up his plate, go back to his den and shut the door. We wouldn't see him again until the next night. None of us were allowed to disturb Dad in his den, not even Mom.

The only time our whole family saw each other was at this table for Sunday dinner. Dad would be here, and Mom, and we would all sit around the table trying to avoid eye contact while Mom served us and picked up our plates like a servant. If she sat down at all, it would only be a second or two before she got back up to do something else. From the time we moved to this house when I was six years old, that was really the only time we would all be together.

The silence is thick at the table, so I run my finger around the rim of my crystal water glass. A deep tone rings through the dining room, like a moan in a tunnel. Dad clears his throat loudly. I put my hand in my lap and bunch up the linen napkin.

"So, Ellie," Candace says as she sets down her wine glass, "Tom tells me that you're a bartender. Where do you work?"

I look over at Dad, but he's staring intently at his mashed potatoes. I'm surprised that Dad has told Candace that I work in a bar. He hates that I never went to college. He told me one Christmas Eve that he just can't picture me in a smoky bar in the middle of the night with a bunch of lowlifes. He thinks I should be married to a guy like him with a real job and a life. Dad's a computer programmer. One of the best in the business. Spends all his time in the world of BASIC and ANSI.

Dad glances at me and catches me staring at him. I immediately look down at my plate. He doesn't look at me often, but when he does, I have to look away. His eyes are ice blue, practically the same color as his shirt. Toby and I call him the Iceman. After we moved to this house, the few times we saw Dad, he would look at us with those eyes, and we could feel the coldness shooting out of them, freezing us in our tracks.

Funny thing is, when I was really young, his eyes weren't cold at all. They were warm. Dad's eyes would laugh and play and light up around the edges. I've been thinking a lot lately about how until I was six Dad would play eight-tracks of Beethoven in the living room in our first house in Pine Bluff, where Dad grew up. Toby, who's two years younger than me, says he doesn't remember this, but I know that Dad and I would spend hours playing "symphony." He said to pretend we were the instruments in the orchestra. He said that you had to be loose, you had to let the music take over, you had to let go of everything and just be the music. I would step onto his long bare feet, and he would hold my hands, and we would symphony all over the room. Sometimes we'd be the flute, other times the violins. My favorite was the piano. I'd close my eyes and try to be the music as his long legs lifted me up and down slowly as if under water, and then bounce me around like I was on a trampoline.

Then one day we stopped doing it-- the day Mom and Dad shut their bedroom door for hours while Toby and I played on the living room floor. I put my ear up against the door, but I could only hear the muffled sound of Mom's voice. When they finally came out of their room, both Mom and Dad's eyes were red and puffy, and Dad walked out the door and didn't come home all night. Mom sat me and Toby on her lap and told us that everything was going to be all right, that we were moving to Little Rock and getting a new house. Later that night I crawled out of bed, pressed my ear against their bedroom door, and listened to my mother cry.

For weeks after that night I begged Dad to symphony with me, but he just looked at me with eyes gone from warm to cold and told me he didn't have time. I finally just gave up. After we moved to this house in Little Rock, Dad opened Digital Systems and started working eighty hours a week.

I used to know all this happened, but lately I've been thinking that maybe I made it all up so I wouldn't have to see Dad as he really is. I guess that's why I'm here again this year, to see if Dad really is how I remember him, or only how I want to remember him. I just don't know anymore.

I look up from my plate at Candace and force myself to smile. "I've been bartending for a year now at White Water Tavern. Have you ever been there?"

I feel Dad glare at me, but I stare intently at Rudolf's nose. Sometimes I just can't help myself. Dad knows I know that Candace has never been to White Water. It's a hole in the wall downtown on the side of the freeway where bikers hang out. It's one of my favorite places in the world. We have live blues bands seven nights a week, not the kind of bands with guys with big hair and tight jeans traveling from one town to the next in a raggedy van. Hair farmers, Toby calls them. No, we get old guy bands from tiny Delta towns who are synonymous with the music they play. Our biggest sellers are Pabst Blue Ribbon in a can and Jack Daniels up, and there's parking at the front door for Harleys only. My regulars have names like Little Joe, Mountain Man, Pinkie and Tomcat. My first night there they nicknamed me Princess.

I'm sure Candace has been to Shug's or The Capital Club or any of the other big-money and fast-talking bars in Little Rock that I wouldn't step foot into. Hell, she probably met Dad at one of those places. But Candace wouldn't be caught dead in White Water. I know this, and I know Dad knows I know it. I wait for Candace to answer.

"I can't say I've ever been to White Water. I worked with a girl once at the Clinique counter at Dillard's that used to go there. She was too wild for my blood, though. No, Tom and I go out a lot to Shug's. That's a special place for us. That's where we met, you know."

Candace turns her head dramatically towards Dad and smiles the goofiest smile I've ever seen. How predictable my dad is. Candace is about five years younger than Rachel, wife number three, who was about five years younger than Caren, wife number two. My mother is the only wife who was Dad's age. I think that's why he left her.

I follow Candace's sappy gaze and look at Dad. He's smiling at Candace, but there's no warmth in his eyes. Candace stands up slowly, says something about dessert, and walks into the kitchen.

This is the first time in years Dad and I have been alone together. Last year Rachel never left Dad's side for one second. I can see why that marriage didn't last very long. The year before was some in-between-wives girlfriend who hired a caterer to make dinner. There were three or four people around at all times. The years before that Toby and I kept cutting jokes that Dad refused to laugh at.

I take a deep breath. Dad is staring at his plate and pressing his fork into his candied yams. I know this moment of privacy won't last long, and I know I won't get another one for a long time. I stare at my dad as he looks down, trying to recognize him from when we would symphony. I want to identify the dad I remember with the man who is sitting at the head of the table. I want him to acknowledge that it did happen and that he remembers and still thinks about it. I want to be six years old again and take off my shoes and feel the music flow through Dad's body and into my own.

Dad's fork stops moving, and he looks into my eyes. For a second I think that twenty-two years have melted away and the dad I remember is sitting at the end of the table. But then I blink, the illusion is gone, and I realize that the Iceman is staring into my eyes and saying something.

"Ellie, why don't you help Candace with the dishes. I've got to make a phone call."

I look away as Dad stands up and walks out of the room. I feel like a child again, not the child who would symphony with her dad, but the child who would dig and dig in the backyard for the buried treasure that was never there.

I stand up from the table and set my napkin down on my plate. I feel so foolish that I can't even bring myself to be civil enough to say good-bye to Candace. I quietly get my coat from the hall closet and walk toward the back door, the tears just beginning to blur my vision. The door to Dad's den is closed tight as I walk past it, but I can still hear the fire crackling in the huge stone fireplace.

As I step out into the cold night, I zip up my jacket. For a moment I think I hear the haunting first notes of Beethoven's Fifth beating in the night air, soft as a whisper. As if they are coming from inside someone. As if they are coming from inside me.

I turn and look at the house, and for a split second I think I see Dad's shadow in the den window, his hands up in the air. I take a step toward the house. The shadow disappears.

And all that's left is the flickering of the fire against the curtains.

I open the car door and sit inside. The engine starts up with a cough, and I turn the radio on as loud as it will go. I don't look again at Dad's house as I pull out and drive away, my whole body beginning to shake.

Tom stands erect in front of the fireplace, his untucked blue button-down fluttering behind him as his body trembles with anticipation. His eyes are closed as they always are, thick headphones encasing his ears, his bald head glistening in the firelight, a thin line of sweat beading above his upper lip. For a moment there is a hush of silence that falls like a velvet curtain, and then Tom's hands rise, pause, and jerk four times with splayed fingers. The orchestra bursts out four ominous notes in C Minor-- and stops with the punctuation of Tom's closing fingers. Again, silence, and then again Tom's hands wrench from the orchestra the four haunting notes as if Fate is knocking at the door. Silence, with the punctuation of his fingers. With the nod of his head the violins begin their lonely cry as the cornets, piccolo, flutes and oboes pick up the haunting movement. Tom creates the music as the harmonies and melodies blend together and course through his body as if they are his breath, his life. The music swells and falls, lives and breathes, whispers a story of tragedy that transforms into triumph in the C Major fanfare of the finale. Every cell in Tom's body pulsates, harmonizes, with the music. He pulls the notes out of the air with his hands and then puts them back with his breath. He forgets where he is as the orchestra performs and tears run down his cheeks. The symphony is him, and he is the symphony.

elizabeth

deep sleep

Elizabeth rocks back and forth on her white back porch swing, the shiny chains creaking like crickets on a summer night as the wind rustles the pines that encircle her house. Her one-year-old daughter Ellie sleeps in her arms, the baby's smooth ivory face nestled against Elizabeth's chest, her tiny hand curled around Elizabeth's finger. Elizabeth can feel her daughter's warm breath through her cotton sundress, and for the hundredth time today Elizabeth feels the warmth in her belly rise upward and spread through her body. She hasn't gone to the doctor yet, but she's known for two days that a new life is forming within her. She breathes in deeply, feeling Ellie breathe with her, and exhales slowly, as if exhaling is not enough to let go of the breath.

Ellie squeezes Elizabeth's finger and shifts on her breast. For a moment Elizabeth fears that she has awakened Ellie, brought her out of her dreams. This is Elizabeth's third pregnancy; she had only been pregnant five months when she lost her first one. It was the summer after high school with a guy she met at a Jefferson Airplane concert. She was still living at her parents' house and trying to figure out what she was going to do with her life. At first she didn't want to believe she was pregnant, so she waited for two months to get her period back. When it didn't come back, she finally went to a doctor across town to get a pregnancy test. She didn't tell anyone. By December she was starting to show, and at the end of the month she woke up one morning on blood-soaked sheets. Her mother called her a whore as their live-in maid Violet rubbed the blood stains on the mattress over and over with a damp sponge.

Since August 23, the day Elizabeth brought Ellie home from Pine Bluff General Hospital, Elizabeth has held Ellie against her heart as much as she can, trying to give her daughter the warmth she never felt from her own mother. Elizabeth can't remember her mother ever holding her close. All she remembers is Violet kissing her cheek and pulling the covers up to her chin. Elizabeth's mother and father were rarely at their home in Memphis, and when they were, they locked themselves in their bedroom suite for days at a time. The trays of food Violet left outside the bedroom door would sometimes go untouched for hours. When Elizabeth was in the tenth grade, she brought her first date home to meet her father. When she opened the front door, her father was passed out on the living room floor, naked, the brown liquid from a bottle of Scotch seeping into the tan carpet. Elizabeth laughed lightly and walked past her father to see if her mother was in the kitchen. When Elizabeth turned back around to see where her date was, the door was wide open and he was nowhere to be found. Elizabeth is now twenty-two, and her husband Tom is the only man in her life who has met her parents since.

Elizabeth glances down at Ellie's face and sees that her daughter is still sleeping. For the first time today, she allows herself to glance across her backyard to her brother-in-law Joe's house. Joe is twenty-six, three years older than Tom whom he treats like a son.

Joe owns MacAnelly Construction, and his wedding present to Tom and Elizabeth two years earlier was this two-story house that nestles up to Joe's backyard, the back porches no more than twenty yards from each other. The closest neighbors are a half-mile away. Joe designed the Victorian-style home himself, an exact replica of his own. Joe's wife, Carley, helped Elizabeth pick out the pastel pink of the bathrooms, the mustard yellow of the kitchen, and the kelly green of the living and dining rooms. Elizabeth's eyes stop on Joe's empty porch swing swaying lightly in the breeze.

Elizabeth again feels the warmth in her belly rise upward, but this time it gets stuck in her throat. She knows that Joe is home right now. He's always home in the late afternoons while Tom is at the office and Carley is at Tots Day Care. Since April Elizabeth watched from her swing as Joe labored in his garden, his thick hands embedded in the dark soil. For three months she has sat in her swing, Ellie in her arms, and watched as Joe gently dug in the soft, moist earth, and then placed seeds into the holes.

Watching him, Elizabeth realized there was something in Joe that she missed in Tom. Tom is always fixing things, gluing together his mother's chipped antique china, untangling a knot in Elizabeth's dainty gold chain he gave her for their first anniversary, popping the soft arm back into Ellie's babydoll. But Joe has the ability to touch the earth and the plants as they grow from seeds to green stems reaching upward.

At first, Elizabeth watched Joe silently. Then, as the weeks passed, she longed for him to acknowledge her, to connect with her like he connected with the soil. She often wondered if he knew she was there but didn't care, like talking about sex with a child in the room.

These afternoon hours were the only time that she and Joe didn't talk directly to each other, as every night Joe and Carley were at her house for dinner, or she and Tom were at theirs. Even when

Joe and Elizabeth did talk, however, she felt there was something between them that could not be said.

Then, four weeks ago on a sticky afternoon in July, Joe stood up from his garden and turned toward Elizabeth. He raised a soiled hand in her direction. His mouth was drawn tight, and his hand twitched, as if he was struggling to keep it down. Suddenly Elizabeth's heart raced. Should she wave back? Or should she look away and pretend not to see him? Abruptly she flushed and felt ashamed. She pulled Ellie closer and breathed deeply.

Then Joe looked down, dropped his hand, and knelt back on the ground. His body was still and his head was down, and for a moment Elizabeth felt fear race through her body. Joe shook his head slowly and turned his attention back to his garden. Elizabeth's face burned as his fingers touched the delicate okra plants.

Elizabeth felt as if she was moving underwater as she stood slowly, placed sleeping Ellie in the basket on the porch, and walked down the steps into her backyard. As she walked through the pines to Joe's garden, she stopped kidding herself. She didn't love Tom. She never loved Tom. She'd only known Tom for three months when he proposed, and she'd wanted to have a chance at a normal family. She'd been living a lie for the last two years, and in order to live at all she would now have to live the truth.

Joe looked up as Elizabeth crossed the invisible border that ran between their backyards. Elizabeth knew as soon as his eyes met hers that the defenses they had built up were gone. She didn't say a word as she stopped, reached down and slipped off her sandals, and then stepped onto the moist soil of the garden.

Joe was kneeling, and as she walked up to him he reached out and encircled her legs with his arms, his coarse whiskers rubbing against her thighs. The sun beat down on her face as they made love in the garden. Joe's hands touched her as if she was one of his plants.

The sound of Ellie's crying finally made Elizabeth look up from the crook of Joe's arm. She had to get back to her daughter. As she sat up, she pulled her sundress into her lap. Joe's callused hands sent shivers up her spine as he brushed the soil from her naked back. They hadn't said a word to each other, but Elizabeth didn't feel the need. She didn't even think about what came next. All she knew was that she was in love with Joe, and that he loved her, too. Whatever was to happen would happen, and they would live through whatever they had to in order to be together.

Now, on her porch, staring at Joe's empty backyard, Elizabeth swallows the burning in her throat. The tomatoes are coming up nicely, the spiny green vines lacing through the stakes and dangling plump red skins. Since that day four weeks ago, Joe has not been back to work in his garden. Elizabeth waited for him every afternoon. Every day at three-thirty his truck pulls into the driveway and out of sight. But his backdoor has not opened.

Elizabeth feels like she hasn't slept in weeks. Nights are more unbearable than days, because when he sleeps, Tom holds her so tightly she is unable to untangle herself. She used to yearn for the security of Tom's arms. But after she and Joe made love, Tom seemed to hold on tighter and tighter each night.

Then, one night two weeks ago, Tom's arms fell away, and Elizabeth tiptoed across the hardwood floor of her second-story bedroom to glance at the full moon. Suddenly her knees felt like water. Joe knelt in his garden. Just as she reached for the window latch, Tom rustled in their bed. His low voice echoed through the room. "Elizabeth, honey, what are you doing? Please come back to bed." Elizabeth's hand lingered on the latch for a moment. If Joe would just give her a sign, she would go to him right then and they could start their lives together. Or, better yet, she would turn to Tom and tell him that she and Joe were in love and that she was leaving him. She knew how difficult it would be for Joe to tell his brother. If

Joe would just signal her, she would take the pressure off him, tell Tom as gently as she could, and then this silence could be broken.

Joe stood up and wiped his hands on his jeans. Then he turned and walked back into his house. Elizabeth's hand slipped from the latch as Tom said, "Sweetie, please. You know I can't sleep without you." She felt the silence envelop her like a glove as she crawled silently back into bed and Tom's arms.

Elizabeth looks down to Ellie's face now and her daughter's eyes flutter open. She runs her finger along Ellie's forehead, the child's skin silky and warm. She knows that Ellie will be awake soon. As her finger traces Ellie's eyes and cheeks, Elizabeth thinks of how, for the last four weeks, she was certain Joe hadn't told his brother about them yet because he was waiting for the perfect time. She convinced herself Joe hadn't come out in the afternoon hours because he loved her too much to see her. She knew by the way his eyes couldn't meet hers when they were with Tom and Carley, and the way he walked away from her if they were alone together. She knew by the way his words sounded strained when he had to speak to her at dinner, and by the way she saw him staring at her two nights ago from his kitchen window while she was washing dishes. She thinks how she brushed his hand last night in the hallway, and his voice trembled as he whispered, "I can't do this." She waited for him to add "right now." It would have made all the difference in the world. But he walked away.

Ellie's eyes are open now, the once baby blue irises starting to turn the deep brown of Elizabeth's. Elizabeth feels like she, too, is coming out of a deep sleep as she closes her eyes and holds Ellie tightly. She doesn't know how she could have been so stupid to think that just because she was in love with Joe, that he loved her, also, and would change his life for her. She doesn't know how she could have sat out here for weeks, waiting for some sign that would never come. She doesn't know how she could have done this to

Tom, who loves her more than anyone ever could. And she doesn't know how she's going to keep this secret hidden deep inside her.

Today she won't wait for Joe any longer. As the sunlight beams down on her, she feels a new strength, as if it is burning away what she has felt and thought and done.

Tom will be home in an hour, his stories full of frustration with his job. Elizabeth will tell him of the new baby, her eyes never leaving his face, the secret buried deep within her. He will laugh and cry and hold her close, tell her how much he loves her and how happy he is. She will tell him she loves him, too, and how she needs him and Ellie. And she will be more sincere than she ever has been, because they are all she has.

Elizabeth stands up from the porch swing, Ellie's cries muffled into her breast. Her face is hot and her hand steady as she reaches for the door and pulls it open. For the first time since April, Elizabeth steps into her house with Ellie in her arms and doesn't look back as the screen door slams behind her.

ellie

overlapping

Big black eyes stare at the corners of the room as the tiny head bounces up and down and the front legs rub together like some mad scientist delighted with his new concoction. I stare hypnotically at the fly on my plate, his long snout shooting out of his face and nibbling on the crumbs of my finished meatloaf. It's Friday, I have a night off at the bar, and here I am at my mother's apartment, bored. Right now I just wish I was somewhere else doing something else besides staring at the renegade fly in her otherwise immaculate apartment.

Yesterday Mr. Potts, Mom's apartment manager, called to tell me that he saw her driving around and around the parking lot for over an hour. We both live in Little Rock, and I try to call every now and then and even come by to see her once a month or so. I moved in with her today. My roommate left last month, and I couldn't afford another month in my own apartment, so I figure I would stay here with Mom until I get back on my feet. It's getting harder and harder to strike out as I get closer to thirty, but the idea of two old maids in a one-bedroom apartment makes me claustrophobic.

I tear my eyes away from the fly and look around the small room. Mom moved to this apartment eight years ago when my father left her and my younger brother Toby went off to college. I left home the year before, twenty and tired of curfews and rules and muffled conversations behind closed doors. When Mom moved in, the complex was called Harrison House and was full of newly divorced women and their fat cats. Somewhere along the way Mr. Potts painted the complex a pale shade of salmon, raised the rent two hundred dollars, and changed the name to Whispering Pines. Then he cut down all the pines to make room for a new parking lot. That's when the divorcees started disappearing, either getting married again or finding a cheaper place and taking their leftover furniture and fat cats with them. But not Mom. She stayed on like a trooper, haggling Mr. Potts every month to keep her rent down and befriending all the new administrative assistants and retail managers who moved in around her. Some of them even call her "Mom," though I have reservations about who would adopt my mother as a surrogate parent. Must be some lonely people out there. It's not that Mom's a bad person. It's just that she's not playing with a full deck. A box of hair, that's what Toby calls her.

My eyes bounce around the room as I hear Mom open and close the oven door over and over and over again. The kitchen and the living room are really one room with a half wall dividing the tile from the carpet. The kitchen table is a card table with a linen tablecloth, and the chairs all have my grandmother's embroidered cushions on them to soften the seat. A green velvet couch takes up the whole wall under the only window, and two antique end tables shine cherry red in the bright light. Mom polishes those tables every night when she comes home from working at Kroger, as if her being gone has somehow dulled the finish. A black and white TV sits alone on a stack of milk crates facing the couch, but I don't think it's been turned on in years. The whole room is about as big as my bedroom when I was growing up.

I finally allow my eyes to focus on the walls. For reasons unknown to me, when Mom moved here she started collecting calendars and sticking them on the wall with multi-colored thumb tacks. Not just a couple of calendars here and there. They cover the walls. There's July 1972 with a Labrador panting in an Uncle Sam hat. November 1965 with a snow capped mountain in the Alps. January 1990 with slender babes in bikinis at Waikiki. Little calendars with a whole year on one page and a stamp from Harry's Hardware on the bottom, and long thin calendars with Chinese characters on each month that reach from the floor to the ceiling. Calendars with strangers' writing on random dates from forgotten years. Calendars on top of calendars, overlapping dates and years and memory and history. Not one of them is of the current month or year or even one of Mom's own. All old, all tossed out with the new year. I just don't get it. I never have asked Mom about this. I don't think I want to.

I look back down to my plate as I realize that the oven commotion has stopped. The fly is gone, probably trying to find a way out of this madhouse while he still can. I pick up my fork (twenty-nine years ago a wedding present with Mom's monogram) and lightly tap on the edge of my plastic plate. The sound is oddly hollow, like a drumstick on a trash can. I look up just as Mom sits down in her chair and sets a microwaved peach cobbler in the middle of the table.

"Ellie, please, could you stop doing that? It's making me crazy."

I place my fork down on the left side of my plate. Mom has this thing about dinner etiquette. If I was to put my fork down on the right side right now, it would send her into orbit. There would be a two hour, one-sided conversation about what silverware goes where. Doesn't matter that there is a plastic spoon sitting beside the silver knife. All that matters is that each piece is where it's supposed to be. When I was younger, I would put my silverware down in the wrong place just to see her lose it. But I'm too old for that now. I really don't feel like discussing the rules of the table for the rest of the evening.

Mom reaches over and starts cutting the cobbler in the rectangular cardboard container. Her hands are amazingly small and translucent, the blue veins under the surface of her skin like miniature rivers. And they're always cold. It doesn't matter what time of year it is. Those hands always feel like they have been submerged in Arctic water for days on end. I used to jump every time she would touch me. It's been years since she's tried.

When she gets tired as she is tonight, I can see veins under the skin across her high cheekbones. She is still wearing her Kroger uniform, a pale green smock with a plastic name tag that shouts *Elizabeth MacAnelly: How May I Help You?* in boldface type. I don't know why Mom kept my dad's name. Her maiden name is Brooks. I've wanted to change my name forever. Ellie MacAnelly sounds like a cartoon character. But Mom never changed it back, and eight years later she still goes by her married name. Another thing I don't want to ask about.

"I hope you like this cobbler," Mom says as she gently places a steaming mound on my plate. "They had a special at work, and I bought six for under ten dollars. All they had left was peach, but I remembered how much you like peach cobbler, so I got all the ones left. Maybe next week I'll get some ice cream, and we can have it a la mode."

I look from the cobbler to Mom and smile. I don't have the heart to tell her that I don't like peach cobbler. Never have. When I was young she would spend hours in the kitchen at our old house making all kinds of things, and most of them were damn good. But through the years I fed most of the peach cobbler to Sam The Man under the table. No wonder he only lived to be six years old. His arteries were clogged with cobbler.

"Thanks, Mom," I say as I look around for the fly to reappear. Maybe he can't eat much, but he could at least help me out a little.

"Now, don't be shy," Mom says as she places an incredibly minute serving on her own plate. "You could probably afford to fatten up a little anyway. Boys don't like bony girls."

I take a bite of the cobbler, the sickeningly sweet chunks disintegrating in my mouth. I certainly don't want to talk about my love life with my mother. As if I have a love life. Maybe a one-night-stand life, that's about it. Who needs a guy, anyway? They all end up leaving you in the end. Sex is all a man is good for, and most aren't even good at that.

I swallow as much of the cobbler as I can and wash it down with the last of my water. I can feel Mom watching me, her eyes searching my face for the sign that I love every minute of this. I look at her and smile, the peaches slimy on my teeth. She smiles back, dips her fork into her serving, and touches her lips lightly. We continue this exchange over and over, me choking it down, her dabbing her lips. Eating with Mom takes the place of talking, which is okay with me, even if it is peach cobbler.

When my cobbler is gone, I place my fork and knife across the center of my plate. Mom stands up and begins stacking the dishes on her arm like a professional waiter. "Now you just sit right there while I start some tea," she says as she turns from the table and walks to the sink.

I've always hated this part of dinner. I have to sit here at the table and let her clean up around me. It drives me crazy to watch her do all the work, but if I try to help, she will get pissed and muscle me back into my seat. Mom has this thing about her kitchen. For twenty-one years it was her place to be, something like sacred ground. Nobody was allowed in unless she invited you. Even when she lost her huge kitchen with all the new appliances, she still acted like this tiny kitchen was hers. She's pretty anal about it even today.

I can't imagine not letting anyone into my kitchen. It certainly isn't sacred ground to me. As a matter of fact, I don't think anything is sacred. Why waste all your energy trying to keep things and places yours? Nothing really is yours. It's all common ground. I turn sideways in my chair and rub my eyes until I see tiny white stars.

When I finally drop my hands, Mom is standing right in front of me. Her smock is turned around backwards, and her hands are covered by huge winter gloves. She is staring at me like she doesn't know me. I've never seen her look at me like this. I start to wonder if she knows I'm here at all.

Suddenly I can't breathe. She's just standing there, her eyes glazed over. I feel like I am disappearing on the spot. I don't know what to do. She looks so afraid, like a child lost in the mall. I can taste the peach cobbler coming back up my throat. Does she not know where she is? Does she not know who I am? I stare hard into her eyes, trying to make her see me.

She blinks slowly three times and then holds out her gloved hands. I don't know what she wants. I reach out and awkwardly grasp the gloves. A smile slowly spreads across her face as her eyes move from mine to the wall beside me.

"You know," she says, "it was twelve degrees when we took you home for the first time. So cold I thought you were going to freeze right there on the walk to the car. But I held you close to my heart so that you could have my warmth. I always gave you my warmth."

I clumsily squeeze Mom's bulky gloves, her hands buried deep inside. Tears blur my vision. Why does she pretend not to know who I am? I was born in August. August 23. My brother was born in May. I have no idea what she is talking about. I look away from her and to the wall as the first tear rolls down my cheek. I blink and focus. There on the wall, staring back at me, is a plump baby boy with a noise maker in one hand and a champagne glass in the other. Bright confetti covers his bare skin, and he appears to be sitting on a mound of shockingly white snow. It is January 1991. Written in big loopy letters in the block of Wednesday the First is *Happy New Year, Joyce!*

Suddenly I am angry. Why can't I have a normal mother like everyone else? I am sick of acting like everything is normal when it is obvious insanity. I can feel her cold hands seeping through the gloves. The tears stop. I look back into her face. Her eyes meet mine.

Mom slips her hands out of the gloves and steps back. The gloves feel like they are full of sand. I drop them on the floor. Mom wrings her hands over and over as she stares at the wall and her lips move silently. I feel the anger pushing through my skin like sweat, threatening to drown me.

I want to grab her around the neck, shake her until she gets a grip on herself and starts thinking straight. Then Mom looks from the calendars back to me. Her eyes lock on mine. I try to look away but can't.

I know she sees me now, sees right inside me. She sees my anger, she sees my selfishness, and, most of all, she sees my inability to reach her. Not because I can't, but because I've never tried. I feel my shoulders collapse as the anger evaporates into the air.

Mom blinks once and looks down. Her hands stop wringing, her lips stop moving, and she reaches up to touch her hair. I am exhausted.

In the silence I stand up and take her hands, the pale skin soft and cold in mine. For the first time in my adult life I don't shudder. She feels small and weak as I put my arm around her shoulders and walk her over to the couch. I don't know if it is her or me trembling as we sit down.

Mom lays her head on my shoulder as I put my arms around her. Hours, days, years pass as she mumbles incoherently and I try to keep her warm. The teakettle starts off in an airy whisper and then screams with steam, echoes bouncing off the years.

the channel

At first I think I'm dreaming, the low whine and rapid breaths slipping into my subconscious like a whisper in an empty room. The sound takes me through a pine forest, down an inky river, into a moonlit clearing with smoldering ashes and a thin ribbon of smoke curling up into the glowing sky. It is strangely soothing, this shadowed vision, and as the whine gets louder I struggle to block it out of my mind. But then my eyes pop open, my hands clench onto the blanket, and I realize with a cold start that Scully, my brother Toby's Terrier mix, is in labor on his apartment living room floor.

I jerk up from the couch and fumble for the lamp, knocking over a day-old orange juice glass that shatters on the hardwood floor. The light is blinding, and for a second I can't see anything in the room. But then my eyes focus, and there she is, her tongue hanging out of the corner of her mouth and blood oozing around her tail. She's lying in the open doorway that leads to the hallway where

Toby's bedroom is, as if she didn't want to come in but didn't want to be alone.

I blink and tear my eyes away from her and to the clock on the wall. 3am. Shit. Toby told me that she wasn't due for another two weeks. He found Scully a couple of weeks ago wandering around his apartment complex parking lot. As soon as he pulled up and opened his car door to get out, the brown, wiry mutt ran up to him and looked at him with the saddest eyes he's ever seen. He said that when he saw that she didn't have a collar on, he knew right then that her name was Scully (after Agent Scully on "The X Files") and that he was going to keep her. He was floored the next day when the vet told him that Scully was pregnant.

He had this trip to Roswell planned all year, so he asked me to please dogsit for him while he was gone. I'm staying with my mom right now to save money, and I've been there for the last few weeks. Toby said he would only be gone a couple of days, and that Scully needed someone around. Toby rarely even leaves his apartment, much less goes on an overnighter. I just couldn't turn him down. Look where that got me now.

I throw off the warm covers and step onto the cool hardwood floor. I just crawled onto the couch an hour ago, after getting off my bartending shift, and had finally settled down enough to sleep. It was a little unusual that Scully didn't meet me at the door, but I didn't think too much about it. It was late, and I was tired.

I carefully step over the broken glass and orange juice and reach for my robe.

I kneel down in front of Scully, her eyes staring at me as if there is something I should do. But I've never seen an animal give birth before. I've never even had an animal of my own. When we were kids, Toby had a Jack Russell named Sam the Man, but he always followed Toby around and slept with him, not me. All I ever did was feed him scraps under the table. I've always thought that animals were too much trouble. Hell, I can barely take care of myself.

I want to reach out and touch Scully, but I heard somewhere that you shouldn't touch animals in pain. They might bite you. I don't know if that's true, but I don't want to take the chance, either. Scully's breathing is getting shorter and her whines are getting louder. I feel the hair on the back of my neck stand up.

Okay, take a deep breath, Ellie. Scully's response is probably normal. She is in labor. Women say it's the most painful thing you can go through. But then there's some crazy idea that you later forget all the pain, block it out. I'm pretty sure that I wouldn't block out something like that.

Suddenly I realize that I should get her a blanket or something, help keep her warm. I think I've seen that on TV, get a blanket and some water and maybe something to put the puppies in when they come out. I stand up slowly, my legs still shaky with sleep.

"Stay right here, Scully girl. I'll be right back." I don't know where I think she's going, but I say it anyway.

I step over her, careful not to startle her, and walk quickly down the dark hallway to Toby's room. I figure she'll want the old quilt that she's been sleeping on since Toby took her in that first night. I flip on the bedroom light, look at Scully's bed, and stop.

There, on top of her old quilt, is a tiny, wet mass in a pool of blood. At first I don't know what it is, maybe something that comes out before the pups, so I take another step to get a closer look. The tiny mass is a stillborn pup.

I take two steps backwards, my heel hitting the door frame. I want to look away, but I can't, my eyes glued to the lifeless body. I keep expecting it to move, to whimper, to suddenly take in a deep breath of air. But it just lies there, completely still, the paws curled up around each other.

Scully's whines from down the hall break the spell, and I turn away from the pup. I can't get Scully's quilt for her. No way. But I could get something with Toby's smell on it. That will help her feel like she's not so alone.

I look at Toby's bed. A white T-shirt is flung on top of the unmade covers, right at the foot of the bed. I take three quick steps, grab the T-shirt, and then scurry out of his room and back down the hall. As I gently lay Toby's T-shirt on top of her, I see that my hands are shaking. Scully never even moves.

I need to think. Maybe it's normal to have a stillborn pup, and then all the other ones will be fine. Toby said that the vet had said that this looked like her first litter. I've heard that for women the first baby is always the hardest, and after that it just gets easier and easier. It's probably the same for dogs.

I look closely at Scully's face and realize that there is a pool of drool spreading like a puddle under her mouth. Her breathing is shallow, and her tongue looks white. Her eyes keep on rolling back in her head, the whites peeking out like crescents. And it looks like the bleeding has stopped.

Something is just not right. The fact that she left her own bed in the middle of the night to come into the living room should be telling me something. And it has to have been a while since the last pup, because I didn't hear her whine at all when I came home earlier. And the drool, the blood, the breathing, the whining-- Scully is trying to tell me something, I just have no idea what it is.

Without thinking about it, I reach out and touch her nose. It's as hot as fire. I stand up quickly, step back over the broken glass, and grab the card Toby left me taped to his computer screen. Riverview Animal Hospital is a few blocks from Toby's apartment.

The first ring sounds like it's coming through a tunnel as I sit down on the edge of the couch.

Second ring, still no answer. But the card says after-hour emergencies, so surely someone will pick up.

After the third ring a cheery female voice says, "Riverview Emergency, how may I help you?"

I quickly explain what's going on, trying to sound calmer than I feel.

"How long has it been since she had the stillborn?"

For some reason I look at the clock and then back at Scully. "I don't know. At least two hours. But I don't know because I just got in from work and fell asleep. An hour later she was in here, whining and bleeding."

"Okay, give me your name and number. Dr. Rich will call you right back."

I give her my name and number. I hang up the phone, my hand lingering on the receiver.

In less than three minutes Dr. Rich calls back, his voice groggy but controlled. He tells me to meet him at the hospital in ten minutes. I breathe in deeply as I hang up. I've got to remain calm.

I can hear Scully's heavy breathing as my robe falls to the floor in a puddle of cotton. I pull on jeans and a T-shirt, my hair coming to life with static electricity.

I slide on my bare feet into clogs. Then it hits me: I have to pick Scully up. I know I should move, but suddenly I can't. All I can think is that she may bite me or start fighting and not let me pick her up. Damn, Toby. Why did this have to happen on the one night all year that you are actually out of your apartment?

But surely Dr. Rich would have told me if I was in any danger. Scully understands that I need to help her. Hell, she's the one who came looking for help. So she's got to let me pick her up.

Slowly I walk over to her saying, "Good girl, Scully, good girl." I stoop down and put my hands under her back. Her fur is warm and damp in my hands, and she stays limp and lets me slide my hands up under her back and around her belly.

I pause for a moment, and then as gently as possible stand up and curl her into my arms.

I turn and walk slowly to the front door, talking to her softly. I carefully pick up my keys off the coffee table, open the door, and step out into the warm night.

My car is parked right out front, only a few yards away. As I walk through the new grass, all I can think about is that pup back there in Toby's room. I guess when I get back I'll have to bury it somewhere, maybe put a stone or something over the grave so I will remember where it is.

I don't know why I'm suddenly thinking about the dead pup. I should be thinking about birth, not death. Strange how they seem like the same thing all the sudden.

I open the passenger door, trying not to jostle Scully too much. She is amazingly calm. As I set her down in the seat and pull Toby's T-shirt around her, I look down at her face. Her tongue is still hanging out of the side of her mouth and a thin line of drool hangs down from her lower lip, but her eyes are not rolling back in her head anymore. I shut the passenger door and then run around the car, jump in, and start it up.

The street is empty as I race to Riverview, and as I pull into the parking lot there's a truck in front of the door and a figure in the entranceway. Thank God I'm not alone anymore.

Dr. Rich greets me at the passenger door, his thick black hair mashed down on one side, his eyes bright and clear. "I'll take her from here," he says as I step out of the way and he leans into the car. Scully whines as he picks her up.

As I follow Dr. Rich into the building, it hits me that I've never been inside an animal hospital before. The reception area is clean and sterile like a human hospital, but there are posters on the wall of different breeds of dogs and cats, and a bulletin board with pictures of animals and animal necessities for sale. When Dr. Rich opens a door and turns on the light, I can't suppress an image of a human hospital with posters of breeds and pictures of people for sale.

I immediately feel claustrophobic in the small room. There is only about five feet of space between a long table and the walls. A sink, cabinets, and a dorm sized fridge line one wall. All shapes of bottles and gadgets are lined up neatly on the counter beside the sink, and for a second I wonder if we aren't in the staff kitchen. But then Dr. Rich gently places Scully in the middle of the metal table and pulls a stethoscope out of a drawer.

I look at Scully lying on the table. Toby's shirt is soaked in blood, she is quietly whimpering, and her eyes are rolling about. As Dr. Rich places the stethoscope to her heart and feels around her belly, I am overwhelmed with sadness. It must be a lonely feeling, knowing that your babies are in trouble and there is nothing you can do for them. You can only wait and hope that someone will help you.

I reach out and touch Scully's paw as Dr. Rich takes her temperature and again touches her belly.

Dr. Rich looks up from the thermometer and starts asking me how old Scully is, if she's on any medication, and if she's had any health problems in the past. My cheeks burn as I explain to him that she's not my dog, that I don't know any of the answers, and that Toby is out of town. I leave out the part about Toby camping in the desert at Roswell to try to catch a glimpse of alien spacecraft. Dr. Rich stares at me intently, as if he is trying to make a decision about my role in all this.

After a moment of silence, Dr. Rich clears his throat. "This is our situation. She's fading fast. I am going to have to do a C-Section. If we don't act soon we may lose her and the pups both. You'll have to assist me. So I need you to quickly scrub your hands and arms while I get the surgical tools together."

Dr. Rich turns and walks quickly through the door, leaving me alone with Scully. I look down at her and then at the sink. I know I wanted to help, but I don't know if I can stomach a C-Section. Just the blood on Toby's shirt makes me a little woozy.

I look back down to Scully and see that she is trembling. I've got to do this.

I step over to the sink and take off my rings. I scrub my fingers and palms, moving up to my wrists and then to my forearms. Less than a minute later Dr. Rich returns with a plastic bin and stands behind me.

"That's fine," he says, "just rinse really well. I'm going to put Scully under and then we'll get started."

I run my hands and arms under the water as I hear the sound of instruments clinking on the metal table and then the buzz of hair clippers. When I'm sure that all the soap is gone, I turn off the water and dry off with paper towels. I turn back around and face the table.

Scully's eyes are closed, and her nose and mouth are covered with an oxygen mask. All four of her paws are tied to the edges of the table with Velcro straps. The skin on her shaved belly is a pinkish-tan, and I suddenly think of human skin.

Dr. Rich has his sleeves rolled up, and he quickly steps beside me and scrubs his hands and arms. As he dries, he calmly explains what we are going to do.

"I'm going to make the incision and then pull back the skin. Then I will pull the intestines and the stomach to the side, so that I can reach the uterus. After that, I will make another incision in the uterus.

"When I see the pups, I will pull them out, one by one, and hand them to you. Then I will clamp the umbilical cord and snip it. After that is done, I need you to hold each pup over your head with both hands, and then quickly pull it down to waist level. That will mimic the motion of the birth canal, which will force the amniotic fluid from their lungs and cause them to breathe. You'll know it's worked when they start yelping. If there isn't any yelping, then you need to do it again. After they start yelping, you need to pinch them a couple of times to keep them breathing and then place them in this incubator. That will keep them warm while we deliver the rest." He looks at me intently. "Any questions?"

Any questions? What does he mean, any questions? How about what if I get sick and have to run out of the room? What if I can't make them breathe and they all die? What if I'm not a good birth canal and I end up hurting them? What the hell am I doing here in the middle of the night?

"No, I guess not," I say, repeating "birth canal, birth canal" over and over in my mind like a mantra.

Dr. Rich walks over to the other side of the table and picks up a scalpel. The bright overhead light glints off the stainless steel.

When he makes the incision in Scully's belly, I feel dizzy, and I place my hands on the table to keep from falling over. But the more I watch the easier it gets, and by the time he opens up her uterus I can feel the adrenaline pumping through my veins. Suddenly I'm excited about taking that first pup and bringing him into the world.

But that excitement turns to fear as soon as Dr. Rich pulls the first pup out. It looks exactly like the pup still back there on Scully's bed, except that it is covered with a white tissuey film. It isn't moving at all, just curled up.

Dr. Rich hands it to me. As he clamps the umbilical cord and then snips it, the pup stays completely still. Then Dr. Rich turns away from me and goes back to Scully.

My hands are shaking uncontrollably. I hold the tiny body up above my head with both hands and then gently pull it down to my waist. There's not a sound. I hold it up again, about to burst into tears.

Dr. Rich turns his head to me. "Pull down more forcefully, like the birth canal. A quick pull will force the liquid out of the lungs. You can't be gentle with them or they won't breathe."

I close my eyes and pull down quickly. Right when I stop there is a loud yelping, much louder than I ever expected. I feel another burst of adrenaline rush through me as I hold the pup up in front of my face with one hand and pinch him with the other. I grab a towel off the table and quickly wipe him off. He looks just like a miniature Scully.

Dr. Rich hands me another pup, so I place the first one in the incubator. He cuts the umbilical cord, and then I hold the pup above my head and forcefully pull down. This one spits liquid on my shirt and yelps on the first try.

There are six pups total, each one an exact image of Scully. The last one that Dr. Rich pulls out is stillborn like the first. It was hung up in Scully's birth canal. That's why she couldn't deliver the rest of the pups-- the tiny body was blocking the way for the others to follow.

Dr. Rich sets the last pup over to the side on a towel and turns back to Scully, carefully sewing her shaved skin back together. "She's going to make it," he says, never looking up. Scully looks so peaceful lying there, as if she somehow knows that everything is all right.

I feel the tears on my cheeks before I even realize I'm crying, and reach over and gently touch the yelping mass of life squirming around in the incubator. It's been at least two hours since I woke up to the sound of Scully's whining, and I wonder if the sun has come up yet. I wonder if Toby is going to call tomorrow, and how I'm going to tell him about tonight.

I squeeze my eyes tightly and take a deep breath.

It feels like I've been standing here for hours, my feet on the floor but my mind floating around the room. The low hum of Scully's breathing, the clink of the scalpel on the counter, and the whimpering of the pups slowly bring me back to the room. The wet smell of afterbirth floats around me like a familiar mist.

Then I feel something tugging at my hand. I slowly open my eyes to see all of my fingers being suckled.

elizabeth

riches to keep

The grass in front of the Golden Years Manor is just starting to turn the pale yellow of winter, but the leaves have not yet faded. They are still the vibrant reds and oranges of autumn. Even the old chinaberry tree, with limbs that lazily bend to the ground, has not withered with last week's frost.

It's been ten years since Elizabeth pulled up in front of this weathered Victorian building in east Memphis. Her mother had just moved in, and Elizabeth walked down this same path while her ten-year-old daughter Ellie waited in the car. Tom stayed in Little Rock with Toby. Elizabeth's mother stood in the doorway of her room that day and told Elizabeth not to come back.

Today, Elizabeth is alone. She pulls open the door to the Manor and steps into the lobby. A small TV is in one corner of the room, and a dozen shriveled people with drab robes sit on folding chairs, staring at it in silence. Elizabeth tries to picture her mother sitting there, but she cannot conjure up the image.

A nurse in a wrinkled white uniform strolls up to Elizabeth. "Can I help you?"

"Brooks. Mrs. Judith Brooks." It's odd to say her mother's name. Earlier today at the graveside, when the priest said it, Elizabeth looked up for a moment, as if he was speaking of a stranger.

The nurse's eyes soften. "Her room is upstairs, second door on the left. Whatever you don't want, we'll take care of."

Elizabeth nods, mumbles "thank you," and then turns toward the stairs.

When Elizabeth got the phone call two days ago, she felt nothing. She has been waiting for her mother to die for years. She thought that she would feel some great weight lifted off of her, as if her mother passing would somehow release her. But as Elizabeth walks steadily up the stairs, she feels only numbness.

The baby blue carpet in the hallway on the second floor is marred with footprints. When Elizabeth was eight, her mother dropped a wine bottle on the kitchen floor one morning, red wine splattering across the tile. Elizabeth ran barefoot into the kitchen to see what happened. Her mother was sitting on the floor, her robe hanging open. Tears rolled down her mascara-streaked face as she tried to put the pieces back together. When her mother yelled at Elizabeth to go back to her room, Elizabeth carefully walked away, her footprints staining the hall carpet with ruby blotches.

Elizabeth opens the door to her mother's room. A cloud of decay and decomposition floats around her. In the middle of the room is a disproportionately large bed. There is one small window with a rotting plant on the windowsill. A flimsy brown nightstand crouches on the far side of the bed, a drab handkerchief that Elizabeth recognizes as her father's covering the top. When Elizabeth's father died suddenly of a heart attack Elizabeth's sophomore year in college, she stayed with her mother for a week in the house she grew up in. The night before Elizabeth returned to school, her mother sat on the edge of Elizabeth's bed late into the night cradling a bottle of Scotch and told Elizabeth that she never did like her, that she was a disappointment, and that she was better off just staying away from her. Elizabeth got up the next morning and left quietly while her mother slept curled up on the bedroom floor.

Elizabeth walks over to the far side of the bed and sits on the edge. Through the window she can see her car. It looks out of place alone in front of the flaking white picket fence. She wonders what her mother saw from this window all those years.

The bed is hard, and Elizabeth shifts her weight. Her feet dangle off the side. She's not sure why she is here, except for the fact that she's the only surviving family member. Over the years, Elizabeth tried to avoid thinking about her mother. Elizabeth filled her days with the small details of keeping her own family together. Now Tom is remarried, Ellie lives in an apartment across town, and Toby is in his freshman year at college.

Elizabeth looks around the room. The walls are bare, the shelves beside the closet empty. There is nothing in this room that would distinguish it as her mother's, except for her father's handkerchief. When she reaches over to touch it, it feels thin, like an old piece of paper.

The plywood drawer in the night stand opens easily. Inside Elizabeth recognizes a long wooden box that sat on her mother's dressing table beside the delicate perfume bottle from France and the red rouge that smelled like wax. Elizabeth was forbidden to enter her parents' room, but every once in a while she snuck in and put on one of her mother's floppy hats or glided red lipstick onto her pouting lips. Once, when Elizabeth thought her parents were watching TV, Elizabeth was gazing into the mirror at her mother's pearls which she had taken out of the wooden box and put around her neck. When her mother popped into the room, Elizabeth snatched at the pearls, trying to yank them over her head. But they burst in a cascade of white and spun under the dressing table and bed. Elizabeth could smell the Scotch on her mother's breath as her mother grabbed for her. But Elizabeth darted through the door, down the stairs, and into the room of Violet, their live-in maid. From behind Violet's door she could hear her mother screaming as her father threw a glass against the wall.

Elizabeth picks up the box. It's light, as if empty. It has no decoration, no insignia, no marks of any kind on the stained surface. She sets it on the bed. As Elizabeth opens the lid, yellowed pearls roll around the bottom of the box and settle in a corner. Elizabeth suddenly has an image of her mother on her hands and knees picking up the pearls from the floor and putting them back in the box.

She starts to set the lid back on when she notices a tiny silver key is wedged into a corner of the box. Carefully she tugs on the key until it comes free and then holds it up to the light. Suddenly her stomach turns. She tries to swallow but can't.

When Elizabeth was eleven, she was flipping through *Fairies* in the library after school. She stopped on an image of a woman with flowing hair that held a loop with three keys on it. The caption under the woman read, "She who possesses the three keys shall have magic from the deep and riches to keep." Elizabeth was so excited she ran out of the library. She stopped in the corner drugstore and bought three small locks with keys. In her bedroom she made a loop out of a broken ring, hung the keys on it, squeezed the ring back together, and slid it onto a long silver chain. That night, her mother smiled absently when Elizabeth gave her the necklace.

Elizabeth clasps the key in a tight fist. Suddenly she is eleven again and in her room making the necklace. This time instead of giving the necklace to her mother she slides the long silver chain over her own head. The keys tinkle as she dances around the room, the fairy of the rings.

The years wash over her as the key presses into her palm and her arm trembles. She squeezes until her arm aches and her shoulders sag. She doesn't know if it's been minutes or lifetimes when she finally releases her grip and opens her hand. The outline of the key is pressed into her palm.

Elizabeth sets the key back into the box, closes the lid, places the box back into the nightstand and shuts the drawer. Then she stands and walks out of her mother's room.

When she turns to shut the door, she stops, her hand lingering on the knob. Then she reaches up and pulls her mother's nameplate out of its plastic holder. It is cold and hard between her fingers as she walks down the hall and steps out into the crisp fall air.

ellie

pieces of me

The afternoon sun forces its way through the door of White Water Tavern, creating a rectangle of white on the hardwood floor. The door is the only source of sunlight in the building, and I watch from behind the bar as occasional shadows approach from outside, pause for a moment, and then step inside the smoky bar. It's as if with each customer the door exhales a breath of stale air and inhales fresh air. I've never really understood the allure of sitting in a dark bar at three in the afternoon, but my regulars are just starting to trickle in, and I've just come on for my Friday night shift.

I pick up my damp towel and run it along the nicked mahogany bar. If there's one thing I've learned from bartending for the past eight years, it's cleanliness. No more than one butt in an ashtray, bevnaps for every drink, and sporadic wiping down of the bar. For one thing, it gives me something to do so I don't feel like I'm just listening to the conversations on the other side of my bar. Besides, I hate sticky fingerprints all over the wood.

My parents hate that I work in a bar. Or, rather, my father hates it. I don't think my mom even knows what I do. She's always been in her own little world, ever since I can remember, probably the product of trying too hard to keep her marriage to my father together. Between cooking and cleaning, my mother hardly ever spoke directly to my father, at least not in front of me. It was like they passed each other, but never connected. Not surprisingly, my father filed for divorce the day my younger brother Toby graduated from high school. That was eight years ago, but in the last several months Mom's lost it pretty seriously, to the point that she doesn't even know where she is sometimes. I moved in with her in her cramped apartment last month because I needed to save money. At first I was pretty irritated having to move back with Mom, but I have to admit I'm glad I did. She's not that bad. She just gets confused sometimes.

I look up just as some guy in a black felt cowboy hat drops quarters into the old jukebox and "On the Road Again" starts playing. I have the volume control behind the bar, and I keep it pretty low until the sun goes down. Tonight we have The Norris Brothers' Blues Band from Helena, an old blind guy who rips the slide guitar and his sons on bass, drums, and harmonica. They play here once a month or so, and bring in a crowd ranging from bikers to college kids. Personally, I could do without the college kids. They take the quarter back on their beer every time.

I hear the door breathe, and look up just in time to see my favorite regular, Mountain Man, stride into the darkness. He's wearing thick black boots, scuffed black chaps over faded Levis, and a faded Molly Hatchet concert T-shirt from 1978. His gray hair fans down a black leather jacket with a chain on one shoulder. He's got his knife case clipped to his belt loop, and on one hand wears a black leather glove to cover scars from a shotgun blast. He's told me he did time at Cummins for crystal meth, but that was twenty years ago when he was young and stupid. He lives out in the country in a trailer his dad left him and rides his Harley into town every afternoon to White Water. Strange as it may seem, Mountain Man is the same age as my parents.

Mountain Man's chaps rasp as he walks up to the bar and sits down on a wobbly stool. He looks at me and winks, his smile creating deep crevices around his green eyes. "Hey, Princess, how's my favorite barmaid?"

I smile back, holding his gaze for a moment. Mountain Man was the first customer I had here, a little over a year ago. That day he was wearing the exact same clothes he is wearing now, and when he walked in he said, "Well, well, if it's not a princess behind my bar." At first I thought that someone named Mountain Man who fought in Vietnam and had a tattoo of a spider on his palm wouldn't want anything to do with someone named Ellie MacAnelly who grew up at the Pleasant Valley Country Club. I even went so far as to lie and tell him that my parents moved to Dallas and don't talk to me anymore. I don't know why I lied. It just came out that way. All my regulars call me Princess now.

I set my towel on the cooler, reach down into the bin, and pull out a Pabst Blue Ribbon in a can. I place a bevnap on the bar and then set his beer on top and say, "I'm doing pretty good. Just wish I could be out in that sunshine today."

He pulls a crumpled pack of Lucky Stripes out of his jacket pocket, taps out two cigarettes, and then crushes the empty pack in his hand. He then puts one cigarette behind his ear, one in his mouth, and flicks his Zippo into a blue-yellow flame.

"Well, you know that ride I promised you is still pending," he says, smoke pouring from his nostrils. "You just say the word, and we can break out of here and get us some of that sunshine."

I laugh and throw the empty cigarette pack into the trash. Mountain Man has been trying for a year to get me on the back of his bike. It's a yellow and black Fat Boy with a custom extra seat on the back. It's a beautiful bike, but I'm scared silly about riding on a motorcycle, and he knows it. In the third grade our next-door neighbor's son died in a motorcycle wreck, and I've been spooked about two-wheeled machines ever since. Toby got a moped when he was twelve, but I wouldn't step foot anywhere near it. I guess some things you just never get over.

"So," I say, propping my black Converse tennis shoe up on the cooler and resting my arm on my thigh, "you ready for Final Jeopardy today?"

Mountain Man and I watch Jeopardy every day at four o'clock. At first he beat me every time, surprising me with answers for categories like Goddesses and French Sweets. Over the months I've gotten better at it, though. Last May we started trying to keep score, but that turned out to be too much of a hassle when I had to help other customers. So now we just bet on Final Jeopardy, and if I win he takes out my recycling when he leaves at dusk, and if he wins he gets a shot of Hot Damn. It's amazing how many bottles of that stuff I've been through.

"I'm ready, Princess. The question is, are you ready to pour me a shot."

Right as I start to say something like "we'll see about that," the door opens again, exhaling into the sunshine. I look over, expecting to see another regular trying to adjust to the darkness, when I freeze, my hand gripping the bar in front of me. My mother is walking into White Water.

She's wearing a yellow flowered skirt and pink blouse, and a to-go container is clutched in her hands. Her auburn hair is pulled back into a tight bun at the base of her neck. As she steps over the white rectangle and slowly looks around the room, I suddenly have an overwhelming urge to duck behind the bar.

Just as I slide my foot off the cooler, Mom's head turns and she looks right at me, her face breaking into a smile. I stand frozen like a deer in headlights as she walks up and sits right next to Mountain Man, setting the to-go container right there on my bar.

"Hi, Ellie, Sweetie," she says, scooting herself up to the bar. "I got off work early, and noticed that you didn't have a bite to eat at the house. I've never been down here before, so I thought I would bring you some dinner so you wouldn't get hungry."

I feel Mountain Man staring at me, but I just stand there. I have no idea what to say. Maybe if I just don't say anything, she will get up and walk out of here and Mountain Man won't ask me why I lied. Or maybe she'll figure out that something is wrong by the look on my face, and she'll try to play it off, act like she's a roommate or something. What is she doing here, anyway? Mom has never been to any bar that I've worked at. She's never even asked me directions to any bar I've worked at. And this whole thing about dinner--I had dinner with her the first night that I moved in with her, but every other night I've either eaten out or I've been here. The chicken fingers and grilled cheeses have been just fine.

I feel stupid staring at her, but I can't think of anything to say. She's just sitting there, staring into my eyes, that smile still on her face. And Mountain Man is looking back and forth from me to Mom. I've got to get a hold of myself.

Finally the silence is broken with the familiar sound of Mountain Man's low, rumbling voice. "Well, well, well. I'll be damned. If I didn't know any better, I'd say that Princess herself just walked in here and sat right beside me."

Mom turns her head toward Mountain Man, and for a second I think that she may fall off her stool. I don't know why I think that. I've never seen Mom startled by anyone. When I was in the eighth grade we had the pool put in, and every day Mom invited all those sweaty, dirty guys into the house for lunch. When she moved into her apartment after the divorce, she made instant friends with the maintenance guy and still sits out on her stoop and drinks coffee with him. When she leaves Kroger every day after working her shift, she gives her change to the homeless guy who hangs out on the corner of Rodney Parham and Reservoir with a sign that says,

"Please Help. God Bless." So I don't know why she would be startled by Mountain Man. I guess I'm the one who's startled by her.

Mom holds out her hand to Mountain Man. "I'm Elizabeth. Ellie's mother. I just thought I'd drop by and see where my daughter works."

Mountain Man takes Mom's hand in his gloved fist and then places his other hand on top. I try to look away but can't. "Nice to meet you, Elizabeth. I'm Mountain Man. You need something to warm those hands of yours up. Let me buy you a drink."

Mountain Man turns to me and winks, and my gaping mouth flattens into a tight line. Mom pipes in just as he's about to order her a drink. "Oh, no thank you," she says, her hand still in his, "I don't drink." She takes her hand back but turns on her stool to face him. "Can I ask you where you got a name like Mountain Man?"

I've got to find a way to stop this conversation. But my mouth feels like it's full of sawdust. I can't even open it right now. Mountain Man looks away from me and back to Mom.

"My mother named me Jack, but I've been Mountain Man ever since I moved in with my daddy out in the Ouachitas. Since I was around sixteen or so. He was running with the Banditos, and I got all mixed up in that for a while, but then I grew up and Daddy died. Now I'm just a country boy trying to get by."

I feel like my head might explode. Like I'm stuck in some alternate reality. I'm caught in a lie that I never should have told, and now that lie is sitting here making small talk with a biker at my bar.

What does she think she's doing? I never asked Mountain Man about his nickname. All the bikers who come here go by other names. It's just the way it is. In a way I wish that Mountain Man would get insulted by Mom and brush her off so she would leave. It's not that I don't like my mom. I just don't particularly want her sitting here, right now, bringing in my past for Mountain Man to see.

And I don't want to hear about his past, either. Some things are just better left unsaid.

I should be so lucky as to have Mom insult Mountain Man. Quite the contrary. Mom and Mountain Man launch into a discussion about nicknames. I feel like I'm stuck in an invisible net as I pick up my towel and reach out to wipe the bar, feigning interest in a circular water stain that has been there for years. As I rub and rub on the permanent ring, I try to block out Mountain Man's deep voice rumbling about how people shouldn't be named until they become who they really are. How birth names should be temporary. How the person who gives someone his true name is the one who can see him completely, totally.

What the hell is he talking about? Mountain Man has never said anything about this before, and for a second I think that he's just saying that to keep up a conversation with Mom. I look up from the stain, my hand still rubbing, and see that Mountain Man is serious about what he's saying. It's as if he's opening up to her in a way he's never opened up to me.

This is not good. Not good at all. If this goes on much longer, Mom sitting there talking to Mountain Man, then I just may lose it here and now. Sure, I like being called Princess. Hell, until I got out of my teens my arms were too thin, my feet were too long, and my curly hair stuck out all over my head like a red Afro. For years I was called anything but Princess, so even though now I get asked out on plenty of dates and get more attention than I could possibly want, I don't mind having a nickname that sounds dainty and small and feminine. But the whole thing about this being my true self is ridiculous.

Mountain Man takes a deep drag of his cigarette and then stubs the butt in the ashtray. As I reach for the still-smoldering ashes, both Mountain Man and Mom pause, a welcome silence for me. Maybe they are through talking and Mom is ready to go home. As I turn to dump the tiny glowing ashes into the trashcan, I feel them both watching me. I take my time jostling the can so that the ashes won't catch fire and revel in the silence. But it doesn't last long.

Just as I turn back to the bar and try to find a way to get rid of Mom, she looks back to Mountain Man. I set the ashtray on top of the water ring just as Mom's voice breaks the silence.

"Well, I have to admit, I've never thought about this name thing before. Even when I was young, I never really felt like an Elizabeth. It was just too big a name for such a little girl. But when I had Ellie, I knew how much a part of me she was, so I gave her my name. Her birth name is Elizabeth, you know. But I called her Ellie right from the beginning."

Mountain Man is staring at Mom intently. Somehow I know what's coming next, and I have no way to stop it. I just stand there as Mom continues.

"I wonder what my real name would be if I had one. I've never really felt like an Elizabeth, but I also don't know what else I would be. Do you know what my real name is?"

Obviously, if Mountain Man was so moved as to name my mother, he would have from the beginning like he did me. And to ask for something like that-- that's like asking somebody if you look fat in a pair of jeans, or if he likes your new haircut. Of course he's going to tell you what you want to hear, not what he really thinks. If he told you what he really thought he would tell you right away, not wait for you to ask.

Mountain Man is just sitting there staring at Mom. She looks back at him. It's as if she's allowing him to look inside her and find a word that will name her for the first time. As they sit there staring at each other, I suddenly feel sorry for Mom, think how Mountain Man can't find a name because he can't find anything there to go on. The longer they sit there, the more my hands start to sweat. I want to jump in and say something, anything, to make her feel better, make her feel like she can have a nickname, too. But I can't think of anything. Not one word.

Finally Mountain Man clears his throat and smiles. I feel the tension release from my body as he looks from her to me and then back to her. There's something in his face that I've never seen before. He reaches down into his pocket with his gloved hand and pulls out his keys.

"I'll tell you what," he says, as he stands up from his stool. "You go on a ride with me, nothing major, just a jaunt around the block. When we get back, you'll have your name."

I'm completely floored. Not only did Mountain Man just ask my mom to go on a ride with him, but the way she is blushing right around her ears and shifting on her stool, it looks like she is actually considering it. Like she is going to hike up her skirt, wrap her arms around his waist, and ride off on that death machine with a man she has known all of ten minutes. Once again, I am unable to open my mouth to warn her of the dangers. Mom says something to me as she stands up, but I can't hear a word. All I can hear is the sound of my blood racing through my temples and absorbing into my brain like a sponge.

I realize that I can't reach Mom, so I look at Mountain Man, who's standing there waiting for Mom to walk out the door with him. I stare at him as hard as I can. But he won't look back at me, not even a glance. He knows I'm staring at him. I can tell by the smirk on his face. But he won't acknowledge me, won't even act like I'm in the room. Shit, this is really about to happen.

My body finally breaks its rigid stance just as Mountain Man opens the front door and Mom steps out into the sunshine. I feel the breath of fresh air blowing through the room as I run around the bar. The door shuts just as I reach it. I stand there in a rectangle of light with my hands on the door. Mountain Man hands Mom a white dome helmet. My heart is pounding in my chest as she puts a hand on his shoulder and stands on the footpeg, pressing her skirt down in between her legs as she straddles the seat.

I feel fear race through my veins like fire. Mountain Man straddles the seat in front of Mom as she wraps her arms around his waist, her helmet crooked on her head. The bike starts up like thunder, rumbling through the building. I think I hear a customer behind me at the bar asking for a drink, but I never take my eyes off Mom.

I can see her face clearly, her chin resting on Mountain Man's shoulder. Her eyes are shining, her mouth is slightly open, and the familiar wrinkles around her eyes seem to have disappeared. Mountain Man kicks up the kickstand, and suddenly I realize with a jolt that it's not fear I'm feeling. It's excitement. As if I'm the one about to take off.

As Mountain Man turns the bike slowly and I catch one last glimpse of Mom's face, I suddenly know I'm watching a piece of me on the back of that bike, a piece of me I've never seen. It's as if we are the same person for a moment, as if there is no difference between her and me. As if there never was.

I feel the sunlight burning through the glass as Mountain Man pulls out onto the street and Mom's skirt puffs up with the breeze. I can feel the wind on my face as Mom's back disappears down the road, strands of her hair escaping from her bun.

I know that when they get back, Mountain Man will come up with a dainty, feminine name, something to make her feel good, all the while looking at me with that smile on his face. Because he has known it all along.

Ellie. That's Mom's real name.

new born

My mother's hospital room is cold and white, the view from the window a red brick wall. I shift on the hard chair. Last week, Mom was in the bathroom when the doctor told me that the cancer had spread from her liver to her pancreas, stomach, and intestines, and that she had less than a month to live. He told me that I could choose not to tell her this, as hope is the only thing that sometimes keeps cancer patients alive. I haven't told anybody, not even my brother Toby. Mom is forty-nine years old and had another round of chemo this morning.

I've been in this room five minutes, and the only sound I've heard is Mom's retching in the bathroom behind me. She's been hospitalized for three days. The first two I stayed with her the whole time, helping her to the bathroom and watching daytime soaps on the TV suspended from the ceiling. But last night I had to go to my bartending job. This morning I was so exhausted I slept until noon. I moved in with Mom three months ago, and this was the first morning that I woke up and realized she may never come back home. I didn't even take a shower before I raced over here to see how she was.

I shift my gaze from the wall outside Mom's window to the yellow and pink flowers and silver balloons lining the windowsill. It was strange yesterday when these gifts started arriving. The yellow roses with baby's breath and the white peace lilies were brought in by two neighbors in Mom's apartment complex that I have seen maybe three times or so. Some lady Mom works with at Kroger brought in the pink carnations in a blue vase and a white basket with a palm-size Bible. Three other people I've never met brought in assorted bouquets. I didn't know Mom had so many friends.

Even Toby, who only stayed five minutes or so yesterday while Mom was sleeping, brought in the silver Get Well balloons with a green Martian smiling and waving. Toby also brought some hair clippers and put them in the bathroom for Mom. He asked me to tell her that she might feel better if she shaved off the last pieces, goes completely bald. She just smiled when I told her.

I look away from the window to Mom's empty hospital bed. There are strands of her auburn hair left behind on her pillow, and I absently reach my hand up to touch my own hair. I inherited Mom's curly red hair. When I was younger, I spent hours trying to straighten out the springy curls and even dyed it blond a time or two. But eventually I just gave up. I found it was much more trouble trying to make it something it wasn't than just letting it be what it was.

As my fingers wind around a curl hanging over my ear, I hear the bathroom door open behind me. I feel my whole body tense up, as if I am preparing for a fight. I turn slightly on my chair as Mom steps out of the bathroom.

My hand drops from my hair as my eyes lock on my mother. She is looking down at the tile floor, her blue hospital gown hanging loosely off her shoulders. One of her hands holds on to a silver pole with an IV snaking from a clear bag to her arm. I try not to stare at the wispy patches of hair on her head, but I can't tear my eyes away. I swear she looks much worse than yesterday afternoon when I left her. I feel a stab of pain pierce my side, and I look down at her bare feet and clear my throat. She catches my eye and smiles, her eyes glassy like fish bowls.

"Ellie, sweetie, I didn't hear you come in," she says in a quiet voice as she reaches out to hold onto the back of my chair. I want to get up and help her back to bed, but suddenly I feel like a fly stuck on a glue trap. My eyes feel out of control as they bounce back and forth from the top of her head to her pale lips. I start to stand up.

"You just sit right there," she says as she steps past me and sits down on the edge of the bed. "I can do this just fine on my own. All I want you to do is hand me that pink book lying over there under the TV."

I watch as Mom carefully lies down on her bed, her head nestling into the pillow. I don't even look toward the TV, as I know there is no pink book there. For months Mom has been talking about things that never happened, driving around aimlessly, forgetting where she is and who she is. When I learned about the cancer, I tried to blame it on that. But when I really thought about it Mom hasn't been all together for years. She has this strange obsession with calendars, and it seems like she is literally making up memories so that she won't have to have her own. By repeating all these things over and over to herself, she somehow convinces herself that they are real. That way she doesn't have to be who she really is. It scares the hell out of me to think that I could be just like her.

The hum of the head of Mom's bed rising up moans through the room. I clear my throat. "So, what's it gonna be today? 'Days of Our Lives' or 'All My Children'? Or should we go out on a limb and watch 'As the World Turns'?"

I try to smile and try to keep my eyes from staring at her head. I've never seen Mom's scalp before. It's like seeing a part of her that has been there all along, but never revealed. With virtually no hair, she looks like a huge, misshapen newborn.

Mom gets her bed in the position she wants, with her head propped up and her feet slightly elevated. She slowly pulls up the crisp white sheet and then looks back to me.

"I don't care about watching TV today, Ellie. I want that pink book. There are things in there that you need to know. I need you to hand it to me so I can read them."

My heart starts pounding as I look away from Mom and to the small table under the TV. Of course there's no pink book there. There's only a folded white towel and a paper cup with fish on it. I never have gone along with Mom's delusions, mostly because I didn't want to admit that she had them. But the urgency in her voice scares me, makes the hair on my arms stand up. This time it sounds like I'm not going to be able to change the subject. I look around the room for something to pick up.

I stand up, walk over to the windowsill, reach into the basket and pull out the Bible. I turn back toward the bed and hold it out to her.

Mom doesn't reach out for the Bible, but instead turns her head and looks out the window. I just stand here, my hand stretched out to her. I have no idea what to do. She's just lying there, looking out the window, not even acknowledging that I am trying. Then I realize with a shock that she doesn't even know I'm here.

As I lower my hand, Mom starts talking. "You were such a little thing," she says, her voice almost a whisper. "Just four years old. At first we didn't know what was wrong. All you could do was cry and point to your throat. When we took you to the emergency room your tonsils were so swollen you could barely breathe. Before the surgery your daddy promised you ice cream, and when you woke up, all you could say was, 'Ice cream, ice cream,' over and over. I don't even think you could taste it. Your daddy and I sat right there and cried with you with every bite you took."

Suddenly I am four years old and lying in the huge hospital bed as Mom holds out the little pink spoon. My throat is on fire and tears roll down my cheeks, but I open my mouth and let the cold ice cream melt on my tongue. My father sits beside my mother on the edge of the bed, and with each bite Mom gives me, he wipes my chin with a paper napkin. Mom is saying what a big girl I am and how I can have all the ice cream I want.

I blink once and follow Mom's gaze out the window. If someone had asked me my earliest memory, I would've recalled riding my orange bike with the white tassels on the handlebars around and around the driveway when I was five. I didn't even know that I had been in the hospital when I was four. But I know now that I was. And Mom has remembered all along.

I have no idea what to say. I look back to Mom, who is staring at me. Her eyes are no longer glassy, and there is a strange glow to her cheeks. At first I think it's a trick of the light, but then I realize that there's something beautiful in her face, something I don't recognize. It's like I'm looking at the same brown eyes, the same thin nose, the same deeply etched lines around her eyes, but I am seeing them all for the first time. I feel my hands clam up and goosebumps pop up all over my body as I stare at this woman I've never really seen before.

For the first time in my life I see my mother as a person. I see her as she must have looked to my father when he fell in love with her. I see her as the people she works with and the people who live in her apartment complex must see her. I see her as a stranger must see her, that first impression that lingers like a mist.

I sit down clumsily at the end of Mom's bed. I am overwhelmed with how blind I have been all these years. I have spent all my life trying to not be like my mother, and suddenly all I want to be is her. The same person she is trying to run away from.

I turn my back to her as the tears well up. I don't want her to see me cry.

I feel her watching me as I walk over to the bathroom and flick on the light. As I shut the door behind me, I am confronted with the acrid smell of vomit.

The toilet lid clunks as I put it down and sit on it. The sobs come in waves as I pull tissue after tissue out of the box. For a second I don't think I'll be able to stop. Then I lean my head back, take a deep breath, and squeeze my eyes closed.

After a moment I lean down, pick up the tissues, and throw them into the trash can. The tears have stopped. I stand up, pull out the last tissue, and wipe my face. I can feel my swollen eyes under my fingertips.

Just as I turn to leave, I catch a glimpse of my reflection in the mirror. There, staring back at me with the same brown eyes, is my mother's face. Not the face I've been looking at all these years, but the face that I saw just a moment ago for the first time. But no, it's not the exact same face. The lines around the eyes are not as deep set, and the nose is just a little longer. And it is framed by all this hair.

I feel Mom's reflection slipping away from me as I stare into my own eyes. Suddenly I know what I must do.

I stare hard into the mirror as I reach over and pick up Toby's clippers and plug them in. It's as if I'm merging and separating with my own reflection as I turn on the clippers and the buzz echoes through the bathroom. Waves of dizziness roll through me, and I reach out with my other hand and grasp onto the edge of the sink. The buzz deepens to a hum as I press the clippers against my scalp and the first curls fall silently into the sink.

elizabeth

82

circling

From her cash register Elizabeth watches through the plate glass window as the Ferris wheel jerks and then starts up slowly. A young mother and her daughter are alone on the ride. Elizabeth feels her heart speed up in her chest as the Ferris wheel circles to the top and the girl's shiny black Mary Janes kick back and forth in the April air. At the top of the wheel the mother holds her daughter around the waist as the girl reaches up to the wispy clouds, her hands opening and closing as if she is catching the sky and releasing it. Elizabeth's heart slows to its normal pace as the mother and daughter descend around the other side, the girl's pink pinafore dress ballooning with air.

Elizabeth thinks back to a cool October day twenty-two years ago when her daughter was six and her son was four. They were still living in Pine Bluff, and Ellie and Toby had begged her and Tom to take them to the State Fair in Little Rock, an hour away. At first Elizabeth didn't want to go. She said that the kids were too young and there were too many people and noise and trash. Somehow Tom talked her into it. When they got there Ellie ran up to the Ferris wheel, giggling and pointing and squeezing Elizabeth's hand. Elizabeth was scared to death of getting on the Ferris wheel, but she finally agreed.

Ellie was wearing a yellow dress with daisies on it, and she held Elizabeth's hand as they stepped up to the basket and sat inside. When the Ferris wheel started up, Elizabeth held Ellie closely. Ellie giggled and pointed as they rose to the top. Tom held Toby, and they waved from the ground.

Elizabeth looks away from the window and to the clock above the Kroger Customer Service booth. Two minutes to twelve. She has been stealing glances at the Mini-Fair in the parking lot all morning, waiting for her lunch hour. When she got to work this morning, there were dozens of children and their parents running around with yellow smiley-face balloons and bright pink cotton candy, but as the morning heated up the crowd thinned, and now there are only a few stragglers wandering around. That's fine with Elizabeth, though. All she wants to do is take her lunch and sit on one of the folding chairs set up beside the Ferris wheel and watch it go around and around.

Elizabeth stayed up all night last night watching old movies on the Classic Movie Channel. She didn't sleep at all. After getting the news yesterday from her doctor that the tumor in her liver was malignant, she had driven around town for hours. The doctor had said that they would have to start chemotherapy right away if there was going to be a chance of stopping the spread of the disease. But his eyes had not looked optimistic.

At first Elizabeth tried to think of a way to tell her daughter and son. Each of her children had suffered in different ways from the effects of Elizabeth's life; she had tried her best, but she had made many, many mistakes along the way. She knows that it is her fault that her daughter isn't married and doesn't have any close relationships and that her son is reclusive and lonely.   She also knows it's her fault that Ellie has to move back in with her tonight because she doesn't make enough money to make it on her own, and that her son barely speaks to her.   If Elizabeth had just made the right decisions throughout her life instead of the wrong ones, everyone would have turned out okay. But she didn't.

She had decided before she even got home yesterday afternoon that she wasn't going to tell them anything at all. She had lived a lifetime of secrets. She had made the mistake one night years ago of drinking whiskey, something she never did, and in a moment of anger revealing to Tom that she had thought at one time that she was in love with his brother.   Somehow she had stopped herself there; she didn't go on to tell the whole truth about the brief affair and their son being the result of that affair. Tom had walked out of their bedroom and didn't come home until the next morning.

This time she would not reveal any truth. Deep inside she felt as though she wasn't going to make it through this disease, and she didn't want her children to carry the pain and worry for longer than they had to. She had already put them through enough.

As soon as she got home she turned on the old movies. She immersed herself in the dramas, becoming the characters and leaving her life and its realities in her small apartment. Then the sun came up and she showered and came to work.

The clock begins its series of bells as the minute hand clicks onto the twelve. Elizabeth turns and looks to the one-way mirror of her manager's office, trying not to appear too anxious. She's still unsure how to act in this job. Her manager, who's about Ellie's age, sticks her head out of the door, catches her eye, and nods. Elizabeth turns off her checkout light and walks quickly to the employee lounge to get her lunch and clock out.

When Ellie and Toby were still living at home, Elizabeth's job was to keep the house clean and cook three meals a day. Even though her and Tom's marriage had fallen apart years before, Tom had vowed to stay until the kids were grown. Elizabeth had vowed to do whatever she could to keep her marriage together, which amounted to saying and doing whatever she thought he wanted her to say and do. Then Ellie turned twenty and moved into an apartment across town with some friends. Elizabeth could feel time slipping away from her, but somehow still believed that if she said and did all the right things that Tom would stay. He handed her the divorce papers the next June, right after Toby's high school graduation. Elizabeth didn't want to try to take care of the big, empty house just for herself, so she moved into a small, one bedroom apartment just a mile from here. Tom kept the house and got a maid. Elizabeth's mother died the next fall.

Over the next two years Elizabeth tried several different therapists. She didn't like any of them. She was diagnosed with everything from chronic depression to obsessive/compulsive disorder to bipolar disorder. They kept changing her medications over and over; Elizabeth felt like she was on a rollercoaster as her moods looped out of control. She finally just quit taking anything and stopped going to therapy. The last session, the therapist suggested that she join a group for adult children of alcoholics. Elizabeth never went. She didn't see the point in continuing to bring up the past. She had messed up her life from the very beginning, and talking about it wouldn't change that reality.

The time clock clunks and Elizabeth pulls out her time card and then takes her brown bag from the refrigerator. The other employees have brightly colored coolers and plastic bags for their lunches, but Elizabeth doesn't feel like she can buy something that fancy. She is getting alimony from Tom, and will be for two more years, but she has no savings of her own and no IRA. Even after eight years on her own, she doesn't have any credit. Every transaction she had been involved in during her marriage had been through Tom, and she still feels like she is starting from nothing. She makes minimum wage, which will help out, but she can't afford to spend her money on frivolous things like lunch coolers. But she can afford to walk outside to the Mini-Fair and sit in the sunshine on her lunch hour.

As she steps out into the spring air, Elizabeth feels her heart speeding up again in her chest. The smell of oil and generators surrounds her like a cloud as she walks up to the flashing lights. A clown with a red rubber nose holds out a balloon animal as she walks through the gate, and Elizabeth smiles and takes it. The clown curtsies and claps as Elizabeth walks past him.

Elizabeth feels like she's stepped into another world as she winds around the fair to the Ferris wheel. A girl with a Razorback baseball cap and scraped knees throws a ball and hits the bull's-eye, and a policeman falls into the water. A father aims a plastic gun at a rabbit that pops up from the wall of grass as his son tugs at his pants leg. A man with no front teeth holds out a green dinosaur and says, "Come on, lady, just one quarter in the bottle and Dino is yours." A bumper car squeaks as a girl sits inside and bounces off an empty car.

Elizabeth turns the corner and stops in front of the Ferris wheel. The woman and her daughter are gone, and the huge, metal wheel sits silent and still in the noon sunshine. As Elizabeth holds her head back and looks up to the top, the white basket seats sway gently in the breeze.

She stands there for a moment and then turns and walks to the folding chairs. She feels exhilarated, as if she is about to ride the Ferris wheel. She sits down on the chair and sets her balloon animal on the ground and her lunch on her lap.

Elizabeth takes a bite of her tuna sandwich. A young man with thick sideburns and slicked-back hair leans against the ramp of the Ferris wheel and blows smoke rings that float through the air and dissipate.

Suddenly, from behind her, a child begins to cry. At first the sound is far away, but as Elizabeth chews the crying gets closer and closer. Elizabeth tries to block the sound out, but then her hands begin to sweat and she decides to turn around and make sure the child isn't lost. As she turns on her chair, she lifts her foot and steps down. The balloon animal explodes with a pop.

Elizabeth freezes, the flaccid balloon stuck under her foot. Suddenly she has no idea where she is. She tastes something warm and soft in her mouth, but doesn't know what it is. She smells oil and gas, but don't know where they're coming from. She feels sunshine on her face, but doesn't know what day it is. She sees bright colors and lights, but doesn't know what they mean.

Then she hears the sound of the child crying behind her. She jumps up quickly, her sandwich falling onto the hot asphalt. Ellie is gone. She was just here, riding on the Ferris wheel, and now she has wandered out into the crowd and is lost.

Elizabeth stumbles down the walkway, the balloon trailing behind her. She feels like she is lost in a maze that loops around and around to nowhere. She reaches up with a trembling hand and wipes her forehead. Everywhere she looks she sees yellow. A yellow teddy bear on the wall of a booth. A man with a yellow baseball cap sitting on a bench. A bouquet of yellow smiley-face balloons tied to a post. But none of these are Ellie's yellow daisy dress.

Beads of sweat roll down Elizabeth's back as she stops at a booth and tries to catch her breath. A man with no teeth is holding out a green dinosaur and shaking him up and down. His mouth is moving, but Elizabeth can't hear anything. It's like she's suddenly in a wind tunnel and her whole body is going to be swept away. She closes her eyes and holds onto the edge of the booth as the wind circles around her like a tornado. She's got to find Ellie.

Elizabeth feels like her head might explode. Then she hears the man's voice swirling toward her. She takes a deep breath and opens her eyes. He is standing right in front of her, his hands empty, his mouth saying, "Lady, you all right?"

Reality slams into Elizabeth like a truck. The man with the green dinosaur is holding it out to her and saying, "Here, just take this. You need to go sit down." A boy with a plastic baseball bat is standing beside her, staring at her. She works at Kroger, and she is at the Mini-Fair on her lunch hour. Tom has left her, Ellie and Toby are grown, and she has liver cancer and maybe six months to live. And she can't tell anyone.

Elizabeth stands up straight and smoothes her hair back with a trembling hand. Her fingers brush across her damp cheek, and she realizes that she's crying. She reaches over and takes the dinosaur that the man is holding out to her, whispers "thank you," and then turns to walk back to Kroger. As she steps back through the entranceway, the Ferris wheel cranks up behind her, the huge wheel jerking and groaning as it begins its first turn.

ellie

take off

"Let's do a drive-by of the old house, Ellie," Toby says as he pulls his arm back in the window and turns the radio down.

It's Sunday morning, two weeks after our mother's funeral. I woke up at eight to my brother shaking me and insisting I get out of the apartment. I crawled out of bed and pulled on a T-shirt and shorts while Toby paced in the kitchen. At first we started out just driving around the outskirts of Little Rock, but before I knew it Toby was heading south toward Pine Bluff, where we lived until I was six and he was four. I don't know why he ended up going this direction-- neither one of us has even been to Pine Bluff for years.

I glance at him sideways, rub my hand over the top of my head, and look back at the highway. I shaved my head right before Mom died, and now it's rough like sandpaper. The lines whip by us in a streak of white.

"I don't think that's such a good idea," I say, as an eighteen wheeler breezes by us, shaking his old Landcruiser. "Why would you want to go by there, anyway?"

I make it a point not to think about Pine Bluff. We moved to Little Rock when I was six. My dad grew up in Pine Bluff, and when we lived there he would sometimes tell stories about him and Uncle Joe when they were kids, but then he stopped talking about Uncle Joe or anything else at all. Now we barely even speak. Toby and I are his biggest disappointments.

I don't know much about Pine Bluff, other than the memories that drizzle through my mind at odd times. Toby has told me that he doesn't remember anything.

"I don't know. Probably just curiosity. Let's drive by and see what it looks like now. Maybe it will jog my memory."

I stare out the windshield as the green exit sign for Pine Bluff comes into view. Now that Mom's gone, Toby wants some sense of where he came from. He wasn't even with her at the end. I sat with her by myself while the breaths slipped away. I guess he wants to make some kind of connection now. But he should've while Mom was alive.

Toby puts on his blinker to get off on Cherry Street. I roll up my window.

At the end of Cherry Street Toby turns left on Country Club Road. It looks the same as I remember from twenty-two years ago, tall white pillars and green striped awnings. I remember my fifth birthday at the swimming pool with hot-dogs and Cokes and mothers in brightly colored swimsuits. My mother sat by herself under a white umbrella.

"Does it look the same to you?" Toby asks as he pulls onto Pleasant Tree Lane.

I take a deep breath and let it out slowly. "Pretty much the same, except everything is smaller than I remember. Are you seriously trying to tell me you don't remember anything? I find that hard to believe."

Toby is silent for a moment. "Nothing looks familiar. If you would help me out a little instead of snapping at me, maybe I would recognize something."

If I would help him out. What about his helping me out when Mom was sick? I'm the one who stayed at the hospital for the last week sleeping on the cot. Toby only popped in in spurts. I'm tired of helping out.

"You're solo on this one, Toby. You're the one who wanted to come here, remember?"

"That much I do remember." He leans his head back and laughs.

We are quiet as we slowly drive down Pleasant Tree Lane. The house is at the end of the road, a half-mile or so ahead. Uncle Joe and Aunt Carley lived right behind us. When they died in a car wreck on the way back from a weekend gambling trip to Tunica, I remember Dad crying for weeks. By the next spring we had moved to Little Rock.

I reach down and turn the radio off as the front of our house comes into view. Our house and Uncle Joe's are still the only ones out here. I can feel Toby's excitement as we pull up to the driveway.

Though the trees are bigger and there is a For Sale sign in the front yard, the house looks exactly the same. I feel like we are kids again and coming home, and I don't want to be here anymore.

But Toby stops the car and jumps out.

"Toby, what are you doing?" I ask through clenched teeth. He doesn't answer me until he shuts the door and leans his head back in the window. His eyes are twinkling.

"I'm going to walk around the side and look. I don't see any cars. Even if people do still live here they're probably at church or something. I want to see the house close up. Come with me."

He's really getting on my nerves. But I don't want to sit by myself. I take a deep breath and follow.

I feel like I am in some strange dream as I walk up to the house. The white lace curtains are pulled back in the front windows, and as I walk toward the side of the house I catch a glimpse of the wooden banister that I got caught sliding down when I thought my parents weren't watching. I had to stay in my room the rest of the night.

With each step I take I tell myself that it's not our house anymore, that I'm twenty-eight years old, that Toby is grown up and Mom died. But it doesn't feel that way.

I turn the corner into the backyard. There's now a tall privacy fence that separates our back yard from Uncle Joe's. Most of the trees have been cut down, and where there was grass there are now cobblestones. The backyard looks barren. There isn't any patio furniture or potted plants or toys, and it dawns on me that the house is empty. I guess the people who lived here have moved on.

Then it hits me that I don't hear or see Toby. I take a couple of steps forward and look up on the back porch. My eyes graze past two forgotten planters on the floor and to the back door. Suddenly I realize that I am staring at the kitchen cabinets through the screen door. The back door is open. Toby is inside.

I run up the three steps to the porch and quietly open the screen door. I don't know if anyone lives in the house on the other side of that fence, but I'm not taking any chances. I step into the kitchen and wait for my eyes to adjust to the shadows.

The kitchen is just as I remember it, even without the breakfast table and Mom's plants. The walls are faded but still the same mustard yellow. The floor is the same black and white parquet but now there are scuff marks. The knobs on the kitchen cabinets are still maroon. And there's a void in the corner where our refrigerator used to stand.

As I slowly look around the kitchen, it suddenly hits me that I see everything from a whole new angle. I am no longer eye-level with the white-tile kitchen counter, but looking down at it. I no longer have to reach up for the doorknob, but reach down for it. Instead of straining on my tiptoes to put my chin on the windowsill, I can look right out the window. And I am no longer six years old, but my mother's age when she moved away from this house.

As this reality sinks in, all I can think is how I was the only one there for my mother at the end, and how Toby is the only one left for me. And for the first time I understand that I need him as much as he needs me. All we have is each other.

I reach for the kitchen counter to steady myself.

After a moment I open the door, step back out onto the porch, and sit down on the old swing. I suddenly remember Toby and me playing airplane. I was the pilot, he was the co-pilot, and we would swing as high as we could and try to touch the whitewashed ceiling. The memory washes over me like rain.

The screen door slams as Toby steps outside. Toby is quiet now, his shoulders sagging and his eyes searching mine. I pat the seat beside me.

He sits down on the old porch swing. It groans under our weight. There is a moment of silence, and then Toby's eyes light up. As I lean back on the swing and press with my feet, Toby laughs and yells, "Ready for takeoff!" We both push off as hard as we can, our toes reaching for the ceiling.

About the Author

Paula Martin Morell, MFA, is the recipient of regional, national, and international awards for her short stories and poetry. Her work has also appeared in publications such as *Short Story Journal, New Works Review, Southern Hum, Outsider Ink, The Foliate Oak, Passport Journal, The Double Dealer Redux*, the *Arkansas Women's Journal*, the *Little Rock Free Press*, and *Word Salad*. Three times she's been featured as an emerging writer at the International Conference on the Short Story in English. She is also the founder and Creative Director for A Way With Words Writing Workshops (www.awaywithwords.org), founder and editor of radio show *Tales from South*, and is co-owner of Starving Artist Café (www.starvingaritstcafe.net). Paula lives with her husband Jason and their daughters Annaliese and Sophia in Little Rock, Arkansas, where she writes, teaches creative writing workshops, and teaches college writing classes online.